D1114922

The Race Is On!

As the rest of the journalists filed in and took their places, Frank heard dozens of languages being spoken.

"Ladies and gentlemen, allow me to introduce the top contenders in the Indy Formula One race, ranked first, second, and third: Manion Cristal, Hugh 'The Rabbit' Conney, and Kellam Marlin."

"Manion," Noah called out, firing off the first question. "The rivalry between you and The Rabbit has already hit the headlines. Only one point separates you two right now. Will the winner of this race get the championship?"

"I will be the winner of this race, and I will win the championship," Manion answered in a thick French accent. "So the answer to your question is yes."

The Hardy Boys Mystery Stories

Available from ALADDIN Paperbacks

THE **HARDY BOYS**®

#181
DOUBLE JEOPARDY

FRANKLIN W. DIXON

Aladdin Paperbacks
New York London Toronto Sydney Singapore

First Aladdin Paperbacks edition October 2003
Copyright © 2003 by Simon & Schuster, Inc.

ALADDIN PAPERBACKS
An imprint of Simon & Schuster
Children's Publishing Division
1230 Avenue of the Americas
New York, NY 10020

The text of this book was set in New Caledonia.

Printed in the United States of America
2 4 6 8 10 9 7 5 3 1

Library of Congress Control Number: 2003103456

ISBN 0-689-85780-2

Contents

DOUBLE JEOPARDY

1 Grand Prix Greeting

Joe Hardy took a seat on the pit wall and unloaded the black portfolio that he'd received during the press orientation. When he heard the distant *vrooooooom* of the first Formula One car on the track, he stood up. He shielded his blue eyes against the bright autumn sun and watched the red Ferrari bank around the far corner.

As it came closer, the sound of the eight-hundred-horsepower engine rose in pitch until it became a high unearthly scream. As the car passed in front of him, Joe clapped his hands over his ears.

"Yikes!" Frank Hardy yelled to his brother, throwing him a can of soda. "That sound is unbelievable." Frank was eighteen, a year older than Joe, with dark brown eyes and hair.

Joe took his hands away from his ears and caught the soda. "I've never heard a sound like that before," he agreed. "It's totally different from other race cars. Now I know why they call an F-1 car a techno-tornado."

"It's sort of like a dentist's drill burrowing straight into your brain," a man said, walking up to join them. "Check your press kit. I think you'll find these will help a lot." He pointed to the earplug in his ear. He wore a badge that identified him as Noah Carter, a reporter for a local television station.

After introducing himself, Noah hoisted himself up to sit on the wall next to Joe. He looked like he was about thirty. He had short, light brown hair and a big smile.

Frank and Joe started flipping through dozens of brochures, pamphlets, tourbooks, and guides to find out where they could eat, shop, and have fun. Several schedules in their kits outlined all the activities planned around the official Formula One Week.

All the Grand Prix teams had contributed press kits about their driver, car, and team personnel. The Formula One organization and the Indy track provided booklets that outlined their histories. Dozens of companies had given promotional items, including complimentary sunglasses and sunscreen, Grand Prix hats, ballpoint pens and notebooks, rolls of film, power bars, water bottles, and loads of coupons and passes for restaurants, theaters, clubs, museums, and other sports venues around town.

"Hey, look at this," Joe said, pulling out a clear plastic bag. "My own set of official Formula One earplugs!"

"Is this your first race?" Noah asked.

"No way," Joe answered. "We were here for an Indy 500 a few years ago. It was awesome. And we've been to some Nascar races."

"This is our first Grand Prix race, though," Frank added.

"You'll have to wear the plugs if you're going to survive the whole week down here in the pits," Noah warned them as another car squealed by.

"I hear you—sort of," Joe said with a grin. He popped the small plugs in his ears.

"So are you print or broadcast?" Noah asked the Hardys.

"Print," Frank answered. "We're student journalists covering the race for the young-adult section of the *Bayport Herald*. I'm the reporter, and my brother is the photographer. We have a special interest in the race because Kellam Marlin, the American driver, is from a town not far from Bayport."

"In fact we set up an exclusive interview with him before we got here," Joe said. "The hometown connection is going to be great for our story."

"Kellam's going to be a real contender," Frank

3

said. "And the owner of his team, Bill Katt, gives a great press party. This year I think the festivities are tomorrow evening. Anyway, the subjects of the real story for this race are Manion Cristal and Hugh 'The Rabbit' Conney. Man, their rivalry is intense."

"I've been reading about it," Joe said. "The Formula One champion each year is the one who accumulates the most points over the whole circuit during the year—and Manion is in first place at this point. If he wins this race, he ties up the championship for this year."

"But Hugh's not far behind," Noah pointed out. "If he wins this race, Manion's got a real fight on his hands."

"So they're pretty fierce contenders, huh?" Frank asked.

"They're total gladiators," Noah said. "You'll see what I mean this afternoon at the press conference. Just putting them in the same room together guarantees a show."

"I can't wait," Joe said. "I've been looking forward to this for six months."

"This is the only Grand Prix in America—the only venue for Formula One racing," Noah reminded them, "so there are over five hundred members of the international press here. It's pretty exciting, even for a local guy like me who grew up with the Indy 500."

As Noah spoke, Joe watched a couple more cars

slam around a hairpin curve. It was like watching two-million-dollar slingshots.

"There are up to twenty-five cars at this race," Noah told them. "Each team arrives with one hundred and fifty employees and budgets of two hundred and fifty million dollars. You'll find out a lot more at the press conference this afternoon. All the drivers and owners will be there."

"I'm really looking forward to asking Manion Cristal and Hugh Conney some questions," Frank said. "I'd like to get a handle on the nature of their famous rivalry."

"It should be fun. See you later!" Noah hopped off the pit wall and strolled off.

The Hardys spent part of the afternoon in orientation and other meetings, and the other part exploring on their own. At a few minutes before four o'clock they arrived at the briefing room in the media center.

Noah had saved them a couple of chairs in the front row. As people filed in and out, he identified the important ones. "There are the owners of the top three teams," he said. "The guy in the suit is Kristièn Savanne, owner of Manion Cristal's team, from Monte Carlo. The one in the turtleneck and cashmere pants is Brian Michaels from Great Britain. He owns Hugh Conney's team."

"We recognize the one in the jumpsuit," Frank said. "That's Bill Katt, Kellam's owner."

As the rest of the journalists filed in and took their places, Frank heard dozens of languages being spoken.

"Ladies and gentlemen, allow me to introduce the top contenders in the Indy Formula One race, ranked first, second, and third: Manion Cristal, Hugh 'The Rabbit' Conney, and Kellam Marlin."

The three racers strode in like thoroughbred horses, confident and proud. They walked onto a raised platform and took seats behind clusters of microphones on a long table. Each man was accompanied by a small group of people who stood nearby.

The moderator made sure that Kellam sat in the middle, separating the other two. Manion and Hugh stared straight ahead, avoiding each other's gaze.

Joe elbowed his way through the crowd of photographers, into a prime spot for shooting some photos. Perpetual camera flashes added to the bright light already created by television spotlights.

"Manion," Noah called out, firing off the first question. "The rivalry between you and The Rabbit has already hit the headlines. Only one point separates you two right now. Will the winner of this race get the championship?"

"I will be the winner of this race, and I will win the championship," Manion answered in a thick French accent. "So the answer to your question is yes." He was about Joe's height and build, but had dark brown wavy hair that hung down the back of his neck. He flashed a broad smile and nodded at the crowd.

Reporters fired more questions from all corners of the room. Frank had to shout to be heard. "A question for Mr. Conney," Frank called out, checking his notes.

"Mmhm?" Hugh mumbled, looking in Frank's direction. "What is it?" He had large dark eyes and a cap of short dark red hair.

"You had a terrible accident in Monte Carlo," Frank said. "Have you fully recovered?"

"*I* did *not* have a 'terrible accident' in Monte," Hugh responded in a clipped British accent. "I was rammed off the track by the thug at the end of this table." He stared straight ahead, not even blinking.

Manion leaned back in his chair, balancing on the two back legs. He looked toward Hugh and chuckled. "You crashed because you are incompetent," Manion said, "and everyone here knows it."

Hugh stomped to his feet with such fury that he knocked his chair over. His eyes seemed to darken as he spoke. "I was winning that race," he said gruffly, "and *you* took me out."

When Hugh stood, another man stood as well—one who had been crouching next to Manion's chair and eating a candy bar.

"Who's the guy eating chocolate?" Joe whispered to Noah.

"That's J. J. Quinn, Manion's timekeeper. "He's kind of a hothead, and very protective of Manion."

"He looks pretty tame right now," Joe said. J. J. calmly chewed the chocolate, keeping his eyes on Hugh.

"That accident was your fault," Hugh said to Manion, "and you know it."

"Still the same whining," Manion said to Hugh. "Give it up, Bunny Boy."

Hugh stood up in a fury and stormed around the back of the table toward Manion. J. J.'s face puffed up with rage, and he stepped into Hugh's path. He threw the chocolate bar down and planted himself with a wide stance.

"Afraid to take me on yourself?" Hugh said, arching his head around J. J. to address Manion. "Sending someone else to do the dirty work? You're not so tough without a car shielding you, are you?"

Reporters chattered into their mics in a babble of languages, describing the action on the platform. Photographers snapped what seemed like a thousand shots. Some of the other people on the platform began to move carefully away from the men.

Hugh dove to get at Manion, but J. J. held him off. A few punches met their mark, though, and before anyone could stop it, the platform turned into a frenzy of flying fists. Within moments, J. J. was knocked off the platform by one of Hugh's

8

mechanics. He landed right in front of the Hardys and Noah.

Noah helped him up. "Hey, J. J., how's it going?" Noah asked with a crooked smile.

The spiderweb of tiny red veins on the side of J. J.'s nose darkened to purple. He pulled back his arm, clenched his fingers into a huge hairy fist, and rammed it straight ahead. Noah ducked just in time, and Frank felt a rush of air coming toward him. He ducked away and raised his hands to deflect J. J.'s punch, but he was too late. J. J.'s fist slammed into the side of his head.

Every one of Frank's senses responded. The blow blasted through his ears with echoing waves of pain. His eyes slammed shut, and neon lights in weird shapes played on the inside of his eyelids. His skin first tingled where J. J.'s fist had landed, then quickly started to pound with pain. A faint smell of chocolate tickled his nose, and he could taste the blood that leaked from the cut on his tongue where his teeth had clamped down.

2 Shakedown to Sabotage

For a few seconds after J. J.'s powerful punch, Frank thought he was going to black out. He forced his balance back, though, took a breath, and straightened up to his full height.

J. J.'s fist pulled back again, but this time Frank was ready. As J. J. punched, Frank raised his arm and caught J. J.'s forearm in midair. They stood there for a second, their arms crossed like swords. Frank could feel J. J. give a little. With one quick blow, Frank knocked J. J. to the floor.

"Nice shot, bro," Joe said, joining him.

"Agreed," J. J. said, grinning up at them. He pulled himself up. Frank and Joe both prepared to defend themselves, but J. J. just nodded and strode off to rejoin Manion's group.

All attempts at bringing the crowd under control seemed only to increase the chaos. Members of the drivers' teams continued slugging away at one another. A steady whir of video cameras mixed with the thuds of punches. The few people who tried to break up the fights soon became targets themselves. Reporters frantically scribbled notes, and the room blazed with photographers' lights.

"Hey, you guys okay?" Noah asked, joining the Hardys. "Frank, you took quite a punch."

Frank rubbed the large knot on his temple. "Yeah," he answered. "I—"

Frank was interrupted by the door slamming open. A mob of track security officers and police flooded the room.

"Come on," Noah said to the Hardys, beckoning them toward a door in the back corner. Frank and Joe followed Noah across the room and slipped through the back exit door.

"Great!" Joe said, looking around the small parking lot. "We got out of there just in time."

"You guys hungry?" Noah asked. "I've got time before I report to the studio. How about some pizza?"

"Sounds good," Frank said, wiggling his jaw to make sure it could still chew pizza crust. His head was throbbing, but his stomach was growling. As the three headed toward the Hardys' van, they heard someone call them from behind. "Hey, hold up a minute."

Frank, Joe, and Noah turned to see J. J. running toward them. He held out his hand as he approached Frank. "Hey, man, I'm sorry," he said. "I'm J. J. Quinn, timekeeper for Manion Cristal. I was out of line in there. No hard feelings?"

Frank nodded and shook J. J.'s hand.

"Cool," J. J. said. He looked relieved. "You know," he added, smiling at Frank, "you pack quite a punch. Where are you all headed?"

"We're going to Maria's."

"Great!" J. J. said. "I'm buying."

They all climbed into his SUV and rode downtown to Maria's. After they'd ordered pizzas and sodas, they sat in silence. Joe figured they all felt awkward because of what had gone down between Frank and J. J. He decided to break the ice. "So it looks like everything we heard about the rivalry between Manion and The Rabbit is true," he said, grinning.

"The point is that it's more than a harmless rivalry," J. J. said. "Competition's great—it spurs us all on. You're not going to have a Grand Prix without drivers pushing their limits and challenging other drivers. But this thing between Manion and Hugh goes way beyond that."

"Okay," Noah said, "So what's your side of the

story, J. J.? I've heard a million versions, but I haven't gotten yours yet."

"Hugh Conney is out to *bury* Manion," J. J. said. He leaned back to allow the waiter to place the huge pizzas on the table. "Hugh's been sending warning notes and making threatening phone calls for weeks now," J. J. continued. "I'm talking serious threats here—not minor jokes or pranks."

"The Rabbit's really been doing this?" Frank wondered. "Are you sure?"

"Well, we don't have any actual evidence linking him to all this," J. J. admitted. "The notes are printed in block letters, and the phone voice is obviously disguised."

"What do the messages say?" Joe asked.

"They're bad," J. J. answered. "They say that Manion is going to crash here at Indy, that he'll be killed. They say he'd better pull out of the race or he'll be sorry. Stuff like that."

"Is there any concrete reason why you think it's Hugh Conney doing this?" Noah asked.

"Who else would it be?" J. J. yelled, flinging his arm wide in a gesture of frustration. "Who'll benefit if something happens to Manion? Who's just nuts enough to do something like this?"

"But isn't it kind of risky for The Rabbit to be involved in threats of this nature?" Frank asked. "I mean, he's a rich man, a champion—an international star. Seems dumb to throw it all away by taking such a chance."

"Taking chances is in his blood," J. J. pointed out. "Drivers like these guys live to take chances. Plus, the bad blood between Hugh and Manion goes way back. They've had a long history of fierce competition. It's built over the years."

"I remember reading about some rough run-ins a while back," Joe said.

"Hugh caused a bad accident for Manion in the Grand Prix at Monza, Italy, four years ago," J. J. explained. "Then Manion forced Hugh out of the Monte Carlo Grand Prix last year. It was pretty obvious he was to blame. Formula One just isn't big enough for both of them."

"Now they're numbers one and two in the rankings," Joe said. "This race has a lot riding on it."

"Have you told the police about the threats?" Frank asked J. J.

"Sure," J. J. said. "But as you pointed out, there's no real evidence that links Hugh or anyone on his team to them. The police basically say we've got nothing. I guess we have to wait until something else happens—maybe another accident—before we can press charges."

"Maybe we can help," Frank suggested.

"How?" J. J. asked.

"Joe and I are investigative journalists," Frank

said. "We could look into the threats and see if we can find out any more information. We'll be around the track all day, close to the action. We might pick up something the police have missed—some thread they don't have time to follow."

Frank flashed a warning glance toward his brother. He wanted him to know that Joe shouldn't say that they were actually amateur detectives. It was a familiar look, and Joe picked up on it immediately.

"That would be great," J. J. said, wolfing down a big bite of pizza.

"Count me in too," Noah said. "I'd love to be the first to break a story like this on the tube."

Frank thought for a minute. He knew that he and Joe worked better without an extra person involved, and he didn't really know Noah. But he also knew that having a local reporter could cut some corners and give them contacts and information that could really help.

Frank looked over at Joe, who gave him a brief nod. "Okay, Noah, you're in," Frank said.

"Excellent," J. J. said.

"The police probably have all the evidence to date, right?" Frank asked. "Can we at least get copies of the notes and phone threats?"

"Absolutely," J. J. replied. "I'm on it. You'll have them tomorrow. Hey, would you guys like to watch the shakedown run from our pit?"

"Are you kidding?" Joe said. "We'd love it! We worked the pit for an Indy 500 a few years ago. It was one of the best times of my life."

"It depends on when it is," Frank said. "I've got an interview in the morning, and I have to be at the Velodrome tomorrow evening for practice."

"Is that for the bike race?" Noah asked.

"Right," Frank said.

"No kidding," J. J. said. "You're racing at the Velodrome Thursday? Man, I wish I were going with you. I wanted to get into the race. My schedule's just too heavy."

"You're a cyclist?" Frank asked.

"I was an alternate for the Monte Carlo team in the Tour de France a few years ago," J. J. answered. "It was so great. I haven't done as much track racing—just enough that I know I'd like to do some more."

"I've never raced at the Velodrome here, but I hear it's world class," Frank said.

"They hold the Olympic trials there," J. J. pointed out. "That's one of the reasons I wanted to give it a ride this year. I'll be in the stands, at least," he added. "I might be too booked for training and racing, but I can take a little time to be a spectator. I couldn't miss it. That and the party for the Children's Burn Center are two of the best activities of the Grand Prix."

"We volunteered to work the party," Joe said. "I'm looking forward to it."

"It should be particularly good this year because of the dinosaur exhibit," Noah pointed out. "These animals are like nothing you've ever seen. The party's right at the museum, in the middle of the exhibit. The kids will love it."

"So will I," Frank said.

J. J. reached in his pocket. "Can you be at the pit at ten-thirty tomorrow? We'll be through by late afternoon." He wrote something in a small notebook, then tore out the paper and signed it. He handed it to Joe. "This will get you past security. Just show the note to the paddock guard, and he'll point you to our pit."

Frank and Joe took the paper and returned to their hotel. It was about ten o'clock by the time they got to their rooms. The teens worked a while on an article about their first impressions of the U.S. Grand Prix before closing Frank's laptop and falling into their beds.

Wednesday morning was bright and cool. It was the first time Frank had really felt autumn in the air. He was glad he'd worn a heavy sweater over his T-shirt, but wished he'd brought his windbreaker. Breakfast was pancakes prepared by a pack of Boy Scouts in a tent in the track infield.

"We told Kellam we'd meet him at nine for the interview," Joe said. "We'll still be able to get to Manion Cristal's pit by ten-thirty, right?"

"Absolutely," Frank said. They quickly finished their breakfast and walked to the paddock, the large area that contained the team garages and suites. The Paddock Club was located on the first turn of the track.

"Mr. Marlin and Mr. Katt are expecting us in the Paddock Club," Frank told the paddock guard. The man checked a list on a clipboard, then ushered the Hardys through. Driver Kellam Marlin and team owner Bill Katt were waiting for them.

"Hey, there," Kellam greeted them warmly. He had sun-bleached hair and a rosy tan. "This is my team's owner, Bill Katt."

"Please, call me Bill," the owner said. "Kellam thinks a lot of you two. I understand you're practically neighbors in the Bayport area."

"Just a few towns apart," Frank said, shaking Bill's hand.

"Well, I'll stay out of the way," Bill said. "Let me know if you need anything."

"Actually, I want to start with Kellam," Frank said. "Then I'd like to ask you a few questions."

"A few photos first, though," Joe said, taking out his camera. He shot some photographs of the two men. Then, while Kellam and Bill answered

Frank's questions, Joe took some more candid shots.

Frank talked with Kellam about his career and his new-found fame as a Formula One winner. They also talked about his chances in this race. "A lot has to do with what happens in the beginning," Kellam pointed out. "This race isn't like other automobile races, with a flying start. In Formula One, we go from a standing start. So a lot depends on what happens then, and what happens right on the first turn."

"I'd like to add a few words about you to the article too, Bill," Frank said. "You are founding owner of KattTEK," he read from his notes, "which is a small research company specializing in identifying and analyzing biological and chemical substances."

"That's right," Bill said. "And although the work my company does is challenging, it's not nearly as much fun as owning a Formula One team!"

"Kellam, one of the big stories in this race is the tough rivalry between Manion Cristal, currently number one in the standings, and Hugh Conney, holding the number two spot," Frank pointed out. "How does that affect you, being right behind those two in the standings? Does it get to you, or can you brush it off and concentrate on your own run?"

"It's hard," Kellam admitted. "But you can't get bothered by it. You have to ignore it and stay focused on the goal: winning."

"The Grand Prix circuit is extremely competitive," Bill added. "It's always been riddled with accusations of foul play and countercharges. But I must say, this race seems to be shaping up to be a little more intense than most."

The Hardys wound up their interview, thanked the two men, and hurried along the track to Manion's pit. J. J. was plugged into Manion's helmet through earphones and microphones. Frank and Joe quickly found their seats next to Noah.

The Hardys and Noah tried to talk to each other, but it was impossible over the noise of the cars. They'd hear a few words, then a car would roar by, interrupting the sentence. They were ultimately forced to give up on conversation and just enjoyed the driving.

Frank watched J. J. pace back and forth in total concentration. Calm and focused, he mumbled words into the thin microphone that angled out in front of his mouth.

Frank watched Manion peel around the turn, then looked back at J. J. Instantly Frank noticed that something was wrong. He could tell by the way J. J. was acting that something was *very* wrong.

J. J. stopped pacing and grabbed his microphone with one hand, bringing it closer to his mouth. With the other hand he clamped the earphone to his ear as if he didn't want to miss one word.

Frank couldn't hear J. J.'s words, but he could

read his lips. He was yelling Manion's name over and over. Finally Frank heard J. J.'s voice.

"He's headed for the wall!" J. J. yelled. "Manion!" he shouted into the microphone. "Manion! Can you hear me?"

As Frank, Joe, and the others watched, Manion's car zigzagged across the track. The high whining squeal grew louder and then erupted with a spectacular, gut-grinding crash.

3 Driven to Danger

While onlookers watched helplessly, Manion's car flipped high in the air, did a backward somersault, and finally landed with a sickening thud.

The track had already erupted with activity by the time the car stopped. The Hardys and Manion's pit crew sprinted down pit row to the site of the accident. Fire rescue crews in chemical-protective gear were already on the scene, flooding the flames with fire extinguishers.

"Whoa! Look at the car," Frank said. His voice was muffled by the hand he'd clamped over his mouth to protect his lungs from the chemicals in the air. The front of Manion's car was twisted into an ugly S.

"He's unconscious," J. J. called out, "but he's breathing!" The rescue team cautiously pulled Manion from the wreckage.

While Frank scribbled notes in his reporter's notebook, Joe snapped photos of the smashed car. At one point track officials tried to push the Hardys away from the scene, but J. J. intercepted them. "They're with me," he said.

The Hardys and J. J. watched as the paramedics loaded Manion into the ambulance. "He's going to the track medical center first, right?" Frank asked. He remembered from his Indy 500 experience that the track doctors were international experts in treating the injuries that plague race drivers.

"Right," J. J. said.

Frank grabbed one of the golf carts, and he, Joe, and J. J. climbed in quickly to follow the ambulance. By the time they all arrived, a crowd had already formed around the medical center entrance. Reporters fired questions at the rescue team as they pulled Manion's stretcher from the ambulance—but the medics didn't say anything.

"Looks pretty grim," Frank said to Joe as they watched Manion being carried into the medical center.

J. J. flashed his ID badge at the security officer guarding the entrance, and he and the Hardys walked into the building. In the corner of the waiting room they found Manion's team owner, Kristièn Savanne.

"J. J.," Savanne bellowed. "This is the work of Hugh Conney, and we *all* know it! Find out exactly what happened. Get the proof we need to show he is a saboteur. I'm going to see to it he never races Grand Prix again!" Savanne barked his orders in short bursts of words.

At last the team of doctors emerged from the examining room. "We can thank the designers of these cars for the good news," the first doctor said. "Manion has no broken bones. He's pretty bruised from top to bottom. His hip was dislocated, but we've repositioned it. He's still unconscious, but we don't see any major problems on the X rays. We're going to keep him here and watch him closely for a little while. Then we'll probably move him to Methodist Hospital for observation for at least one night. No visitors for now."

Track officials, Savanne, and J. J. escorted two of the doctors outside for a press briefing. The Hardys joined the rest of the reporters.

Each doctor took a turn at the microphone. One gave a quick briefing of Manion's condition, and another volunteered to answer a few questions.

"Was it a mechanical failure?" one of the reporters asked. "Did something happen to the car?"

Savanne elbowed one of the doctors aside to

answer. "We are sure that another team is involved, and this crash was a result of sabotage."

The crowd went wild. They shoved closer to the briefing team and started to fire a lot of questions at once.

"Was it The Rabbit? Do you think Hugh Conney caused the crash?"

"Any possibility it was an explosion?"

"Were the tires cut?"

"One question at a time," Savanne pleaded. He motioned for J. J. to step up to the microphone.

"The mechanics are going over the car right now," J. J. said. "It'll take a while to determine exactly what caused Manion to go into the wall. We're not prepared to discuss how this happened at this time."

Again Savanne elbowed his way to the microphone. "As you know, we've had several problems lately," he said, his face red with anger. "And although we cannot prove it yet, we are sure we know who's behind these troubles. We have turned over evidence to the proper authorities. Perhaps after our investigation of this crash is complete, we will have the final proof we need to back up our suspicions."

The doctors and Savanne went back into the medical center, and J. J. motioned for the Hardys to follow. After they managed to fight their way inside,

J. J. answered a few more questions from the journalists. Finally he pulled the Hardys into an empty room and handed Frank a large bulky envelope.

"Here are photocopies of all the written threats and a transcript of the telephone message. The local police have the originals, but they haven't found anything to implicate Hugh Conney. They've checked them over and there's nothing—no fingerprints, nothing from the handwriting, nothing from voice analysis. They *do* think the voice was disguised, though."

"How is Manion?" Joe asked.

"Actually he's pretty good," J. J. answered. "You're familiar with these cars, Joe. Because of all the safety features, he got off with only bruises and the hip thing. He's already yelling about being released—he wants to get back on track."

J. J. moved toward the door. "He's pretty heavily sedated right now—I've got one of the members of the pit crew sitting with him in case he wakes up. Right now I've got to get to the garage. Take a look at the stuff in the package and we'll talk later." With that, he left.

Frank tucked the envelope into his backpack. "Come on," he said to Joe. "Let's find someplace where we can take a look at this package."

It was a short walk to a string of food booths and kiosks. The Hardys picked up some tacos and sodas and found a bench where they could sit for a while. Frank reached for his backpack, then changed his mind when he saw Noah walking toward them.

"I saw you talking to J. J. at the medical center," Noah said, sitting down next to Joe. "How's Manion?"

"Okay," Frank said. He didn't mention the envelope of evidence J. J. had given him.

"Did J. J. tell you anything about the crash?" Noah asked. "Anything that hasn't already been released to the press?"

"Not yet," Frank answered. "He was in a hurry to get to the garage. He's hoping they'll find something when they take the wrecked car apart."

"Hey, Noah," Joe interrupted, "is she trying to get your attention?" He watched a young woman in a blue jogging suit walk toward them. She looked like she was in her mid-twenties. When she was a few yards from the bench, she pulled a small ski cap off her dark blonde hair. Joe recognized the hat: It was like the ones worn by fans of the racing team from Finland.

"Hi, Becky," Noah said. He nodded toward her, then turned to the Hardys. "This is Becky Hannah. She's on The Rabbit's publicity team." He turned back toward the woman. "Becky, this is Frank Hardy and his brother, Joe. They're covering the race as student reporters for the *Bayport Herald*."

Becky flashed a quick smile at the Hardys, then

launched right into her message. "Hugh Conney had nothing to do with Manion's crash," she said, glancing from one teen to the other. "Nothing."

"So you think it was an accident?" Frank asked.

"Probably," Becky answered. "Look, Manion is a hotshot—everyone knows that. He's been known to overshoot a curve before. And he loves to curb." She looked at Joe. "You know those concrete curbs before and after the curves? Well, 'curbing' is when drivers use those curbs as part of the track and actually drive over them," she explained. "And if the driver isn't careful, he can get airborne."

"I know what curbing is," Joe said, going to stand beside her. "I know a lot about racing. I've even driven this track, in an Indy 500 car."

"Other than loyalty to your boss, what makes you so sure no one from The Rabbit's team is trying to knock Manion out of the race?" Frank asked.

"I'm not surprised that they blame Hugh," Becky said. "These guys have a major rivalry going. But Manion's not the only one being threatened. Hugh's been getting warnings too."

"Have you talked to the police?" Frank asked.

"Sure," Becky said. "They checked the notes and answering machine tapes. The identity of the person or people behind them is always disguised. But anyway, those aren't the only problems we've had."

"What else has happened?" Joe asked. He opened a can of soda and handed it to her. She gave him a grateful smile, but her hand shook when she took the can. He looked closely at her and saw an expression of real fear in her eyes.

"One of our shipments of parts was stolen," she told them. "A scrutineering report—with which officials make sure we're complying with the rules—had been forged with fake numbers. The worst thing was when one of the car's gauges was re-set. That could have caused a really bad crash. Everyone on our team believes that Manion is behind it. We just can't prove it."

"I agree it sounds bad," Frank said, "but Manion's the only one who's really gotten hurt."

"Frankly I wouldn't be surprised if Manion set up that crash himself," Becky said.

"Now why would he do that?" Joe said, shaking his head. "That's crazy."

"Because he *is* crazy. He'd do anything to set up Hugh—even crash his own car," Becky said. "If he can implicate Hugh and get him arrested or at least disqualified from the race, Manion erases his only real competition. And he's got the championship in his pocket.

"Manion—or *someone* on his team—is threatening Hugh," Becky asserted. "And we're going to prove it." She put down her can of soda. "Nice meeting you guys," she said as she walked off.

"Cute girl," Noah said, "but blindly loyal to The Rabbit. Well, this break's over. I've got a story to file. Catch you later." He headed across the infield toward the media center.

"So what do you think of Becky?" Joe asked. "She seems pretty sure that Manion's the bad guy here. Even thinks he could have caused his own crash just to set up The Rabbit."

"Sounds a little far-fetched to me," Frank answered. "But this whole competition is really weird. I'd like to get a look at the medical report of his crash injuries, just in case."

"The hospital's still crawling with reporters," Joe pointed out. "Let's go join them."

The Hardys walked back to the medical center. Dozens of people still milled around outside and inside the building. The security guard who had been at the front door was no longer at his post.

Frank and Joe slipped inside and scanned the area. "There's the guard," Joe said, watching a track officer talking to a small crowd of reporters. "It's the same one that was here before, when J. J. got us inside. He might remember us. Just act as if we still belong here."

"J. J. said that Manion's in that room in the back," Frank said, nodding toward a closed door. "I've got an idea. It'll work if I can just get back there without getting stopped. Stick with the guard. Keep him busy as long as you can."

Joe wandered over to join the other journalists interviewing the guard. Frank slipped past and hurried to Manion's door. When he reached the room, a nurse was just going in with a tray of medication.

"Excuse me," Frank said. "J. J. Quinn sent me over to sit with Manion for a while."

"There's someone in there now," the nurse said. "Mr. Cristal is still asleep. Did you clear this with the security guard up front?"

Without answering, Frank pushed the door open for her and then followed her in. He was relieved to see the familiar face of one of the members of the pit crew in a chair by the window. The man immediately recognized Frank.

"J. J. told me you were here," Frank said, thinking fast. "Take a break and get something to eat. I'll sit with Manion until you get back."

"Great," said the pit crewman. "Here's my beeper. Yell if he wakes up. I'll be right back."

Frank sat in the chair and smiled at the nurse. She seemed reassured and placed the tray on the bedside stand. She then changed Manion's IV bag with another bag full of medicine and replenishing fluids.

Frank looked around the room. There was only one bed and one chair besides the one the pit crewman had taken. Near the door was a nurse's station with a sink and a short counter with drawers. Cabinets lined the wall above.

When the nurse finished, she went to the nurse's station and recorded some notes in a black book. Then she placed the book in a drawer, smiled at Frank, and left, closing the door behind her.

Frank waited a couple of minutes to make sure she was really gone, then went to the nurse's station. *It'll just take a few minutes to look through these notes,* he told himself. *You're right by the door—you can hear anyone coming.* He took a few deep breaths as he flipped through the small black book. Finally he found the first report made after Manion was brought in from the crash.

He read as fast as he could, trying to memorize a couple of key pieces of information. It wasn't easy—many of the notes were in the cryptic shorthand that doctors and nurses often use. Suddenly he heard a loud whooshing noise, and he jumped. He relaxed a little, though, when he realized the whoosh was the sound of his own blood pounding through his temples.

The next noise he heard was definitely coming from outside his head. Footsteps tumbled along the hallway outside the room. Frank slapped the notebook together and shoved it into the drawer. He didn't know which came first: the door pushing open or the loud "Hey!" that came from Manion's bed.

4 Chasing the Truth

Frank felt trapped. Manion slowly pulled his head up from the pillow. His head was very wobbly, moving back and forth on his shoulders. "Hey," the patient repeated. "Who're you? What do you want?"

At the same time that Manion spoke, the door pushed open.

"Here I am," said the voice from the other side of the door. Manion's crew member poked his head around. "I'm back. Thanks for giving me the break."

Frank felt a rush of relief flooding through his chest. The crew member didn't seem to find it odd that Frank was standing at the nurse's station. He went straight over to Manion's bed. "Hey, boss, lie back. You're supposed to be resting."

While the crew member calmed Manion down, Frank quietly backed out of the room. He hurried to the front of the building and motioned for Joe to follow him outside.

"I take it you got inside the room," Joe said, joining his brother. "Did you find out anything?"

"Plenty," Frank said. He told Joe about his stint in Manion's room. "And here's the deal," he concluded. "Manion was unconscious *before* he crashed!"

"*Before?*" Joe repeated.

Frank nodded.

"So *he* was sabotaged," Joe said, "not the car!"

"Now all we have to do is find out why he lost consciousness while he was driving," Frank pointed out. "Did he have some physical problem? Or was it something else?"

"Maybe he was drugged," Joe wondered out loud.

"You mean injected with something?" Frank said. "Or do you think someone gave him something in his food or drink before he got in the car?"

"Or after," Joe said.

"What do you mean?" Frank asked.

"A tube in the helmet leads from the driver's mouth to a high-pressure drinking bottle inside the car. When a driver needs fluid, he pushes a lever next to the throttle. The liquid feeds from the bottle right into his mouth."

"So someone could have spiked that fluid," Frank said.

"It's possible," Joe said.

"Think back," Frank said. "When you were taking the photos of the wreck, did you see the drinking bottle? Was it still intact?"

"I didn't have time to check things out," Joe said. "I knew I had to shoot fast before they dragged the car away. Let's go to the media center. I can upload the photos and see what I've got."

Frank and Joe walked across the infield, through the paddock parking lot, and into the media center. Inside, dozens of journalists worked on their stories about Manion's crash. Print reporters clicked away at computers; television reporters recorded voiceovers for the video that cameramen had shot. Photographers checked their closeups on monitors.

Joe found a free computer and began feeding in his photos. While he worked, Frank opened the package J. J. had given him. "Anything interesting?" Joe asked, still watching his screen.

"It's pretty much what J. J. told us it was," Frank answered. "And he's included a note describing the originals. He says they were written in block letters, in black ballpoint pen ink on plain white paper. The threats are pretty explicit, but also pretty standard stuff: 'You're going to die,' 'You'll never finish the race,' 'Get out while you can.' That kind of thing."

He opened another folded piece of paper with typing on it. "This must be the transcript of the phone message. Looks like it's more of the same. It says Manion's headed for a crash at Indy. J. J.'s note says that the phone call was traced to Hugh's apartment in London. The postmark for one of the threats was also London. Another threat was sent from here in Indy, and the third was apparently hand-delivered. It was shoved under the door of Savanne's suite."

When he saw Noah wandering over to join them, Frank put the papers back into the envelope. He met Noah halfway and led him away from Joe's computer. He wasn't ready to include him in the Hardys' theorizing yet.

"I've been looking for you two," Noah said.

"Hey, Noah," Frank said. "What's up?"

"I've been doing some investigating, and I think I've come across something big: a new suspect in the sabotage of Manion's car."

"I'm listening."

"Have you ever heard of Doobie Poliano?" Noah asked.

"Maybe," Frank answered. "Who is he?"

"D. B. Poliano, better known as Doobie, owned a Formula One team several years ago," Noah explained. "The first driver he ever signed was Manion Cristal. Manion had done some small-time racing but had not been very successful. But people who knew Formula One racing could see his potential. Doobie took him on as a rookie."

"Yeah, I remember something about that. I knew the name Poliano sounded familiar. Does he still have a team?"

"No. After his rookie year, Manion jumped to Kristièn Savanne's team—it was flashier and had a lot more money. Poliano went bankrupt within months. For years he blamed Manion for his losses. Then he pretty much dropped out of the scene. No one's seen him for years."

"I have a feeling you're going to add 'until now' to that sentence," Frank said.

"You got it," Noah agreed. "Doobie Poliano has been spotted here in Indy this week."

"And you think he might be targeting Manion?"

"Well, he blames Manion for all his trouble," Noah said. "Seems to me he'd be a prime suspect."

"Have you seen him here?" Frank asked.

"No," Noah said.

"Who has? Have you talked to any of these people?"

"Actually Becky Hannah told me about it. If you want to talk to her, I could set something up."

"Yes, please," Frank said.

"Good. Well, I'd better file my story on the crash," Noah said. "See you guys later?"

"Yeah, maybe," Frank said. "We'll be hanging

here at the track this afternoon. I'll be at the Velo-drome for bike practice this evening."

"Maybe after your session. Are you going to the press party the American team is throwing?" Noah asked.

"Sure," Frank answered. "We'll probably stop by after my practice."

"If we don't run into each other before then, Becky and I will see you there," Noah suggested.

"Cool," Frank said.

After Noah left, Frank went back to Joe and told him what Noah had said about D. B. Poliano.

"I remember hearing about him a few years ago," Joe said. "It sounds like he might be a legitimate lead."

"*If* Becky's telling the truth," Frank pointed out. "We need to make sure he's really been seen and that she's not just throwing that name out to take the heat off of The Rabbit. Remember, she's paid to tell everyone that Hugh is innocent." He looked at Joe's computer screen. "How's it going?"

"Pretty good," Joe said. "It's taking longer than I thought, though, because I'm zooming in on some of the shots and making extra prints."

"Great," Frank said. "The extra time and effort will be worth it. I'm going over to the paddock now to track down J. J. Join us as soon as you can."

Joe nodded, still watching the computer screen.

It took only a few minutes for Frank to get from the media center to the paddock. J. J. was nowhere in sight, so Frank used his cell phone to call him. When he got J. J.'s voicemail, it could mean one of two things: either J. J.'s cell phone wasn't turned on or the line was busy. Frank knew there was no way J. J.'s phone was turned off because he always had to be available to the entire Cristal crew. So J. J. had to be talking to someone else.

Frank left a message and waited for J. J.'s return call. Restless, he paced a little. "This is ridiculous," he muttered to himself. "I'm totally wasting time here."

He checked his watch. Fifteen minutes had passed since he left the message for J. J. He shoved the phone back in his pocket. *I have to be at the Velodrome for biking practice at six o'clock,* Frank thought, *and my bike's at the hotel. Joe should be here in another twenty minutes or so. I'd save time by going to pack up my bike instead of just waiting here. If we get into Manion's garage later, I can stay longer and just leave from here to go to the Velodrome. That's the best plan.*

Frank sprinted to the media center parking lot and the Hardys' van. Traffic was light, so it took only ten minutes to drive back to the hotel. Frank parked in one of the loading zone spots and hurried inside.

The lobby was full of people, most of them standing in a long line that snaked up to the registration desk. In the short time it took Frank to cross to the elevators, he heard seven different languages.

He checked his watch again as he stepped off the elevator. "Looking good," he whispered. "I should beat Joe back to the paddock."

The fifth floor hall was empty. He hurried quietly along the thick carpet. As he approached the room he could see something was wrong. A paper-thin sliver of light outlined one side of the door. Someone had been in his room—or was still there.

His heart began to beat fast. He swallowed hard.

Frank pinned himself against the wall and slid toward the door. He focused all his energy on two senses: sight and hearing—especially hearing. He strained so hard to detect the slightest sound that he realized he was holding his breath. He stopped moving for a few seconds and took a quiet deep intake of air through his nose. Then he started toward the door again.

As Frank got about a yard away from his room, he heard a strange noise coming from inside. It was a scraping sound, like metal against metal.

Suddenly the noise stopped. For a few seconds, a heavy silence filled the hall like a bank of fog. Another sound then trilled through the air. From his pocket, Frank felt the vibration of his ringing cell phone. Pressing his back hard against the wall, Frank watched as the door to his room began to open, an inch at a time.

5 Unsportsmanlike Behavior

Frank's pulse filled his head with sound—almost enough to drown out the trill of his ringing phone. He reached into his pocket and turned it off as the door to his room slowly pulled back.

He looked around the hallway, then darted for the door to the stairway exit. Quietly he pushed the door, slipped through the opening, and crouched down. The top half of the door was a window, so he hid himself behind the lower half and peered through the bottom corner of the window.

As he raised his head just enough to view the hallway, he saw a figure dressed in jeans, a dark jacket, and a cap sidle from his room and pull the door shut. Then the person turned and headed straight for the stairway—Frank's hiding place.

Frank ducked out of sight and backed away from the door a little. The door pushed open, and Frank saw the intruder's leg and arm. Frank waited until the person was halfway through the door before shoving it closed.

"*Whaummmmph.*" A strange sound burst from the person Frank had trapped with the heavy door. It sounded like air being squeezed from a bellows.

Frank released the door a little, just in case he'd done any major harm. The person was still trapped, with an arm and a leg on either side of the opening. "Who are you?" Frank demanded of the intruder. "Why were you in my room?"

"*Mmmm. Uhhnnngg.*" The person groaned and snorted a couple of times, but wouldn't talk.

"Give it up," Frank said. "Or I—" Frank's words were swallowed in his own groan. With a sudden kick, his captive pushed the door back into Frank. Without looking back, the person leaped for the stairs. Frank flung himself forward to tackle the fleeing intruder, but he missed and slammed to the floor in a belly flop.

Frank stood up and was immediately assailed with an overwhelming dizziness. He leaned over to let the blood rush back to his head. Once he shook off the pain, he shot down the stairs, taking two at a time. Somewhere in the stairwell below he heard a door slam, so he stopped at each floor, opened the door, and scanned the hallway for his prey.

After going down a few flights of stairs, he noticed a small metal triangle on the landing next to the door leading to the second floor hallway. He picked it up carefully and dropped it in his pocket. Then he checked the second floor. He found that the hall was completely empty in both directions, and he didn't hear any footsteps.

He continued down the stairs and flung open the door to the lobby. He scanned the large open room, but saw no one matching the description of the man he had pinned in the fifth floor exit door. He'd lost the trail.

He raced back up to his room. At first it looked as if nothing was out of place. The bed was made and there were fresh towels in the bathroom, courtesy of one of the hotel maids. The drawers and closets looked untouched. His computer was still secure.

"Looks like it wasn't a thief," he whispered to himself.

He walked to the small desk in front of the window. Papers and other things strewn on the top were just as he'd left them. As he scanned the surface carefully, though, he noticed something. Hanging off the corner of the desk was a short braided cord. It was gray and about six inches long. He studied it for a moment without picking it up. It didn't look familiar.

Frank called hotel security and reported the intruder. The security officer arrived immediately and took Frank's statement. Then Frank took the silver triangle and the piece of cord and left.

Frank checked his watch. It was five-fifteen. He grabbed his bike and gym bag and hurried down to the van. By the time he got back to the track and parked the van, Joe and J. J. were waiting for him.

"Hey, there you are," Joe called out. "We've been looking for you."

"I returned your call a little while ago," J. J. added. "He says you guys want to see—" J. J. was cut off by his ringing cell phone.

"Yes," J. J. said into the phone. He paced as he talked. While J. J. huddled with the phone, Frank casually led Joe a few yards away.

"Where were you?" Joe asked in a low voice. "You look like you've been in a crash yourself. Your face is all red, and you're kind of limping."

"Yeah, a belly flop on concrete will do that to you." Frank told Joe what happened at the hotel.

"Whoa," Joe said under his breath. "Did you get a good look at the guy?"

Frank shook his head. "I don't even know for sure if it *was* a guy, but I think so. My first view of the intruder was as he backed out of our room. Then when we were in the stairwell, I was behind him—or her."

"No hair color or anything?" Joe prompted.

"No. The person had one of those short pointed caps pulled down over his head—like the ones the Finnish fans wear. Black jeans, dark green jacket."

46

"That could be anyone," Joe pointed out. "Becky even wore one of those hats, remember? They sell those caps at one of the kiosks."

"I did find a couple of things," Frank said, reaching into his pocket. "Do you recognize this?" He showed Joe the short gray cord.

"No," Joe said. "Why?"

"I found it in our room," Frank answered.

"You think the intruder dropped it?"

"Or the maid," Frank offered. "They're the only people who've been in our room since we left."

"We hope so, anyway," Joe added. "You said you found a *couple* of things. What else have you got?"

Frank took out the silver triangle with the hole along the edge. He turned it over in his hand. There were two raised numbers on one side: "1" and "7."

Joe took the object and studied it. "Could be a sort of identification tag."

"Maybe for a safe deposit box," Frank suggested. "The hole might be for a keyring." He took it back and returned it to his pocket.

"Do you think the intruder dropped it?" Joe asked.

"Maybe," Frank said. "It was in the stairwell. It could have been dropped by anyone, really."

"And the cord could be from something the maid uses," Joe said. "We don't have much, do we?"

Frank shook his head. "Did you print all the photos of the crash?" he asked.

"I did," Joe answered. "And it looks like the cockpit wasn't damaged too severely. They design these cars now so that the front end takes a lot of impact. It's amazing."

"Did you see the drinking bottle in any of the photos?" Frank asked.

"I magnified the print of that area. It looks as if it's collapsed, but still there."

"So we could check it out," Frank said.

"If we can get to it before someone else does," Joe added.

"I don't want to tell J. J. anything about this," Frank said. "Not until we know more."

"Are you saying you don't trust J. J.?" Joe asked, lowering his voice even further.

"I'm saying I don't *know* him. And until I do, I want to be cautious. Look, someone targeted *us* today. How many people know we're interested in this whole Manion/Hugh business?"

"Well, J. J., and Noah."

"Exactly," Frank said. "Plus anyone they might have told."

"Right, I'm following," Joe said, nodding.

"So let's keep our suspicions about the drinking bottle to ourselves for now. If we get in to see the car, I'll distract J. J. while you check it over." He glanced in J. J.'s direction. "It looks like he's winding up his call." The Hardys went back to where J. J. was pacing.

"Right now?" J. J. said into the mouthpiece.

"Okay, I'll be right there." He flipped the phone shut. "They're getting ready to shake down the backup car," he told the Hardys. "Plus Manion checked himself out of the medical center. Except no one seems to know where he went."

"Can we get in to see his car?" Frank asked. "Is it in the garage?"

"Yeah," J. J. said. "They picked it up right after the crash and took it straight to the garage. Come on—this'll be a good time to check it out. Most of the team is in a dinner meeting to discuss the backup car. They'll be up in the suite. The rest are out looking for Manion. I'm supposed to wait in the garage in case he shows up there and talk him into going back to the medical center for observation or at least up to the suite to rest." He paused for a moment, then chuckled. "Fat chance."

J. J. eased them through the security checkpoint and they headed straight for Manion Cristal's garage. The garage was locked when they arrived. J. J. unlocked the door, and after the three of them were inside, locked it behind him.

Joe was relieved to see that no one was there. Mechanics had taken apart some of the mangled car, but the cockpit was pretty much intact. It was sitting on a worktable along the back wall.

Joe headed straight for the cockpit. He could hear Frank and J. J. talking behind him for a few minutes. Then J. J.'s ringing phone and beeping pager took over the job of keeping him distracted.

Joe visualized the schematics he'd studied of the dashboard and walls of the Formula One cockpit. Then he started his search. Not only was the drinking bottle missing, but the lever Manion pushed to release the fluid was missing too. *Were they destroyed in the crash?* Joe wondered. *Or has someone else already cut them away?*

Frank joined Joe at the worktable while J. J. talked on his phone. Joe told his brother that the drinking bottle was missing. "My photos show it was in the cockpit right after the crash, so someone's removed it since then," he concluded.

"And was taken from here," Frank said. "J. J. said the wrecker took it directly from the track back to this garage."

"So who removed it?" Joe wondered. "Was it one of Manion's mechanics? If so, it should be over on that other table with the rest of the salvaged parts, and it's not. Maybe investigators took it because they also suspect that Manion was poisoned."

"Or maybe it was the poisoner getting rid of the evidence," Frank suggested.

The Hardys poked around the rest of the garage, checking out bits and hunks of wreckage for the missing drinking apparatus. They found no trace of the drinking equipment.

"Did you find anything telling?" J. J. flipped his phone shut.

"Not really," Joe said, "aside from the fact that some parts of the car aren't here."

"I'm not surprised," J. J. said, looking around the room. "They've been working pretty hard on it since the crash, trying to find out what happened. Everything the crew removed is over on that table."

"I checked there," Joe said.

"Security people have been here too," J. J. said. "And even the police, in case it was sabotage. They might have taken some things."

J. J.'s pager beeped. "Look, I need to go," he said, checking the pager display. "They want me to find Manion. I can't really leave you guys here by yourselves. How about helping me track down the escaped patient?"

"Sounds good to me," Joe said, looking at his brother.

"You two go," Frank said. "I need to get to the Velodrome or I'll lose my track time."

"Okay," Joe said as J. J. answered yet another call. "I'll hang out with J. J. Maybe I can find out more about the crash. I'll see you later at Bill Katt's press party."

After putting in a good two hours of practice at the Velodrome, Frank went to the American team's press party. It was ten o'clock by the time he arrived. He found Joe at the buffet table.

"Just in time." Joe greeted Frank with a sandwich piled high with cold cuts and cheese. "How was practice? You showed 'em who's boss, right?"

"It felt good," Frank said. "I'm pretty psyched about the race. And I'm starving." He heaped some chips and fruit on his plate next to the sandwich his brother had made for him. "How did it go with you and J. J.? Any clue as to where Manion is?"

"Nope," Joe answered. "It's like he just vanished. Do you think something else might have happened to him?"

"I don't know," Frank said. "It's so weird that he's just disappeared."

"You talking about Manion?" Bill Katt asked, walking up. "It's weird, isn't it? I told you this would be a crazy Grand Prix. Where do you suppose he is? The pits are full of rumors."

"I have no idea," Frank answered. "Do you have any guesses?"

"I suspect he went home to Monaco to recover from his crash," Bill offered. "Wherever he is, I'm sure he'll be back in a day or two. He wouldn't miss this race for anything. Are you getting enough food? Please enjoy yourselves. Kellam will be by later." He moved on to speak to an adjacent group.

"Where does J. J. think Manion is?" Frank asked Joe. "He surely has some idea."

"He says he has no clue," Joe said, "but—"

Joe stopped talking when he saw Noah hurrying

up to them. He looked like he'd been hit with a bolt of electricity. His eyes were wide, and he spoke in a low voice, as if he couldn't believe what he was saying.

"Are you ready for this?" Noah said. "Hugh Conney's been arrested."

6 Tracking Trouble

"Arrested?!" Joe repeated. "The Rabbit? What for?"

"I'm not sure," Noah answered, "but it has something to do with Manion Cristal. They took Hugh downtown a few minutes ago. I'm going there myself as soon as I find my cameraman. I'll be right back."

The room erupted with activity as others heard the news. One by one, reporters and photographers put down their plates of food and rushed for the door.

"Have you heard the news?" Becky asked, joining Frank and Joe.

"Yes," Frank said.

"Look, I have to get downtown," Becky said to the Hardys. "But I need to talk to you, and it's got to be private. Let's go outside." She led the Hardys out of the suite and down to a secluded spot near the west stands.

"I've checked you two out," she said, her voice very low. "I know all about your background. You're not only investigative reporters—you're investigators, *period.*"

"How did you find that out?" Joe asked.

"That's my job," Becky said. "I'm in international publicity and public relations. My job is knowing people—who they are, what they do. I have a network of sources all over the world. I know all about your background as detectives."

"Look, Becky—," Frank started.

"Don't worry," she said. "I haven't told anyone else, not even Noah. And I don't intend to if you'd like to stay undercover."

"For the time being, yes," Frank told her.

"Done," she promised. "But, do me a favor. Help me prove that Hugh is innocent. I know that man. Yes, he's very competitive. He's as much of a hothead as Manion, and he's not above a little trick now and then. But he would *never* do anything illegal—anything that would actually keep him from racing. And I honestly don't think he could ever hurt someone. Please help me."

Frank and Joe exchanged looks, then nodded at each other. "We'll take a look at what's going on," Frank told her.

"But you've got to be straight with us," Joe said. "Tell us everything you know, and don't hold anything back."

"I will," Becky assured them. "Now I've got to get downtown. I'll probably be up half the night meeting with the team. Can we get together for an early breakfast?"

"I can't," Frank said. "I'm racing in the morning at the Velodrome. How about lunch?"

"Okay," she said. "Depending on what I find out downtown, maybe I can come to the race, or at least meet you there afterward. We'll have lunch and I can tell you what I know."

"We'll need *everything*," Frank stressed. "I want information about all that's happened to your team so far."

Becky smiled and tried to feign confidence. Frank could see, though, that she was really worried. She hurried out of the room without speaking to anyone else.

"So what do you think?" Joe asked his brother.

"I don't know," Frank said. "I keep coming back to the fact that although both drivers have been threatened, Manion's the only one who was actually hurt."

"And now he's missing," Joe added.

"Right. We definitely need to find out what that's all about," Frank said. "It could answer a lot of this mystery."

"Well, J. J.'s sure that Manion is an innocent victim," Joe said. "And Becky's sure The Rabbit's an innocent victim. But *somebody's* got to be guilty."

"So let's find out which one," Frank said. "We're keeping Becky's request to ourselves, right?"

"Right," Joe agreed. He looked at his watch. "I'm supposed to meet J. J. in a few minutes. He said he had a lead on what happened to the drinking bottle in Manion's car." Joe fished a small card out of his wallet and showed it to Frank. It had a dark gray stripe along one side.

"A swipe card?" Frank asked.

"It'll get us into the paddock whenever we want," Joe said. "J. J. got it for us. He put his job on the line for this, though. If anyone from his team finds out he gave us a card, it could be a problem."

"It's worth the risk to him," Frank reasoned. "He knows that if we can clear Manion, he'll be a hero."

"Does it feel like we have too many 'clients' all of a sudden?" Joe said, grinning. "We've been asked to clear *both* drivers."

"Hey, the more information we get, the quicker we find the truth," Frank said.

"Look, you need to meet J. J.," Frank said. "I'll go to the press briefing about Hugh's arrest. You keep the van, and I'll ride downtown with Noah."

"Don't forget you've got a bike race tomorrow morning," Joe said. "It's already ten-thirty. It'll probably be midnight before either one of us finishes up. Why don't you have Noah take you back to the hotel after the briefing? I'll keep the van. You need to hit the Velodrome at full speed tomorrow."

"Good idea," Frank said, smiling. "I'll give you a call if there's any change. Speaking of my bike, it's in the van. Could you bring it upstairs when you get home?"

"Don't worry—it'll be safe," Joe assured his brother.

"You guys want to ride downtown with us?" Noah asked, walking up with his cameraman.

"Frank will," Joe said. "I still have to work with some photos from the crash."

Joe watched Frank and Noah leave for the police press briefing. Then he walked from Bill's suite to Manion's garage. A couple of mechanics were inside, still pulling apart the wrecked car. They seemed startled to see Joe.

"Hey, who are . . . oh, yeah, you're that friend of J. J.'s." While one of the men addressed Joe, the other stood in front of the wreckage as if to protect it. "You're some kind of journalist, right?"

"A photographer," Joe said. "But I'm not here on business. See, no camera." He held up his hands. "I'm meeting J. J. here."

"He's in a team management conference right now," the other man said. "He'll probably be tied up for a while."

"No problem," Joe said. "I'll just hang around here until he's finished."

The men went back to work, turning their backs to Joe. "So, are you going to be able to salvage anything?" he asked them. "Any parts that can be used in another car?"

"Look, if you don't mind," one of the men said, "we need to get our jobs done here. We'll probably be here most of the night as it is. We don't really have time for chitchat."

Joe could tell that without J. J. around to grease the skids a little he was seen as an outsider. He gave his questioning a rest for about ten minutes, then tried again to start a conversation. But the men wouldn't talk.

Finally, after a hushed conversation between the mechanics, one of them walked over to Joe. "How about waiting outside for J. J.," he said. He guided Joe firmly toward the door and nudged him through it. The door closed and Joe heard the lock turn.

"Okay, then," Joe said under his breath. "Message understood."

He waited for a while, then checked his watch. It was ten-fifty. *I wonder what's going on at Hugh Conney's garage,* he thought. *All the management's probably downtown . . .* He decided to wander over and check it out.

At first it looked very dark inside, with no signs of

activity. The garage had only one window. It was located on the back wall of the garage and was painted black on the inside. Joe stayed in the shadows. He knew that he was even less welcome here than he was at Manion's garage.

As he drew closer, Joe noticed a tiny scratch in the paint blacking out the one window. It was too small to actually see through, but it did glow periodically with a faint light. *That could be coming from some sort of flashing monitor or gauge inside the garage*, he thought. *But maybe not.*

He stepped closer and turned his ear to the dusty window. *There's someone shuffling around in there*, he noticed. *Maybe the person's holding a small flashlight or a lighted match?*

He pressed his ear hard against the black window, holding his breath so he could hear the shuffling noise. The intermittent glow behind the tiny paint scratch suddenly disappeared, and the shuffling sound seemed to get closer.

Joe looked around. It was very quiet, and he seemed to be the only person in the area. He darted behind a parked car near the garage. He could still see the garage door through one of the car's windows.

The stony silence was suddenly pierced by the sounds of voices coming from his left. Joe was breathing very fast now, his chest pumping in rhythm with his heart. He glanced around for a larger shield and spotted a dumpster ten yards away.

As he crept away from the car, he heard a low click—like the turn of a doorknob. Suddenly a muscular arm wrapped around Joe's neck from behind. Joe's knees buckled, and he fought for his breath. He managed to push back up quickly and regain his balance.

Joe tried to suck in some air, but he could feel his throat constrict from the pressure of his attacker's forearm. Twisting and attempting to pull away just made the big arm pull tighter against his throat.

Joe grabbed at the arm with both hands, but it was like trying to pull away a steel rod bolted to wood. The struggle became harder, and finally he couldn't breathe at all.

7 Lights! Camera! Action!

Joe's assailant clenched his forearm hard against the front of Joe's neck. With one last gasp, Joe forced air into his lungs and jammed his elbow back into the person's body.

A groan from behind him told Joe he'd hit his mark. When he felt the slightest loosening of that burly arm's grip on his throat, he gathered all his strength and prepared himself to take the advantage. Leaning forward, he pulled his attacker up over his body. Then with one quick jerk forward he threw the person off his back and watched the body sail through the air. It landed on the ground with a thud.

Joe's legs were still a little wobbly. He leaned

forward again, bracing his hands on his knees, and took in a few large gulps of air. With his brain cleared and his body ready for the fight, he started for his attacker, who was scrambling to stand a few yards away.

Before Joe could grab his assailant, the person bolted down the drive alongside the garage. Joe chased after his attacker, but after a few turns he lost the trail. Frustrated, Joe realized that whoever it was had disappeared into the darkness.

While Joe was snooping around the garages and waiting for J. J., Frank was downtown at the police briefing about Hugh Conney's arrest.

Frank and Noah had parked behind police headquarters and joined the several hundred other journalists who were hurrying inside the building.

"Can you believe the turnout for this?" Noah said, shaking his head.

"Sure," Frank replied. "The majority of these reporters and photographers are from countries other than the United States. In some countries, the Grand Prix drivers are huge heros."

The briefing room was medium size. Frank and Noah took seats toward the front. Within minutes all the seats were filled and reporters and photographers filled all the available standing room.

On the raised platform at the front of the room

sat a long table surrounded by chairs. Several microphones were propped on the table. Various broadcast reporters took turns adding mics from their stations to the cluster that was already on the table. Photographers checked light settings, and television cameramen jostled each other for good positions.

Finally several people filed onto the platform and took seats behind the table. Frank recognized some track security officials. Others wore city police uniforms, and there were a couple of men and one woman in plain clothes.

The police spokesperson introduced herself, then got right to the point. "I know you have heard that Hugh Conney has been arrested," she said. "I'm sure you've also heard that Manion Cristal checked himself out of the track medical center and has since disappeared. We have reason to believe that Mr. Conney has had something to do with Mr. Cristal's disappearance."

Loud whispers filled the room. Reporters who had been speaking quietly into their own microphones in the back of the room began feeding the news in many different languages. Camera flashes blasted the room with bright light. At least a dozen reporters jumped to their feet and shouted questions at the speaker.

"Okay," the police spokesperson said. "Now, we're

going to have to have some order in here, or you can just forget the whole briefing. If you want the information, let me give it to you at my pace. After I've finished with my statement, I'll open the floor to questions."

The journalists seemed to settle down a little. Some sat back down, and the ones who had been giving a live feed to their stations resumed speaking in quiet voices.

"Not long ago Hugh Conney was seen under the west stands of the track having a heated argument with Manion Cristal," continued the spokesperson. "Our witness saw this argument escalate to a shoving match, and Mr. Cristal was pushed to the ground. Then Mr. Conney was seen picking him up and carrying him off to an unknown destination. In an attempt to get a closer view of the scene, our witness moved from a more distant location to a closer one. In so doing, he lost sight of the two drivers and did not see what happened after Mr. Conney carried Mr. Cristal off."

The spokesperson referred to a piece of typed paper, then finished her statement. "On the strength of this eyewitness report, we obtained a warrant to search Mr. Conney's vehicle and hotel suite. Evidence linking him to Mr. Cristal was found. Subsequently we picked up Mr. Conney. He is being held at the moment as a material witness in the disappearance of Manion Cristal—but we expect to file revised charges soon." She put the paper down and looked out at the crowd. "Now I'll take your questions," she said.

"A certain length of time has to pass before a person is declared missing," Frank said. "When was Manion officially declared a missing person?"

"That time is determined by the circumstances of each case. In this one, factors such as Mr. Cristal's physical and emotional condition as a result of his recent accident were taken into account. Added to that was the apparent fact that he was actually picked up and taken away to an unknown location. We have yet to find Mr. Cristal."

"Did Hugh tell you where he took him?" a journalist asked from the back of the room.

"All communication between investigators and Mr. Conney is off limits for questions at this time," the spokesperson answered.

"Can you tell us about the evidence that you found during the search?" another reporter asked in a heavy French accent.

"This case is not closed by any means. It is an ongoing investigation. And I'm not making any comments or answering any questions about the investigation itself, the evidence, or statements made by the material witness."

"Will you identify the eyewitness?" someone asked. "Is it someone involved in the race?"

"We won't identify the person at this time," the spokesperson answered. "I think you can assume that if the witness observed something under the stands at the track, he might have some involvement with the Formula One event." The spokesperson looked over at one of the men in plain clothes, who was shaking his head.

"Okay, everyone, that's it for now," the spokesperson said. "We'll keep you posted about the next briefing."

Everyone behind the table stood up and filed back out of the room, ignoring the shouted questions and calls from the journalists.

"Well, that was quick and dirty," Noah said. "And they didn't offer much time for questioning. It's a pretty slim story so far—but a huge one."

"I'd like to know who the eyewitness is," Frank said as they joined the others who were leaving the briefing room.

"Me too," Noah said. "I hope we find out more tomorrow."

Once outside police headquarters, Frank turned to Noah. "Thanks for the lift down here," he said. "I'll see you tomorrow."

"Come on," Noah said. "I'll give you a ride over to the hotel."

"No, I'd like to walk," Frank said. "It's only a few blocks away."

"Okay. See you tomorrow morning at the Velodrome! I know it'll be a great race."

Frank watched Noah pull away, then headed toward the hotel. As he walked, he tried to call Joe on his cell phone, but he got the voicemail and left a message. He had the same experience when he tried to call J. J.,then Becky.

It was nearly midnight when Frank got back to the hotel. He checked with hotel security, but they had nothing to report regarding the identity of the intruder. As he walked through the door to his room, he was overcome with an eerie feeling, much like the one he had when he'd confronted the intruder earlier.

"Joe?" Frank called. "Are you home yet?" There was no answer. Frank's thoughts returned to the person who'd prowled around the room. *What did he want?* he wondered. He checked the room again for any evidence he might have missed, but he found nothing.

As he showered, he went over the press briefing in his mind. *Is it possible that the rivalry between the two top Formula One drivers in the world has jumped the track to actual crime?* he wondered. *Does Hugh Conney have something to do with Manion Cristal's disappearance?*

Finally Frank tumbled into bed. As he drifted off to sleep, he pushed all the unanswered questions about the case out of his mind. Instead he thought of the bike race the next day and saw himself flying around the Velodrome track to the finish line.

While Frank was walking from police headquarters to the hotel, Joe was driving the van out of the media parking lot at the track. He noticed a dark SUV pulling out of the lot at about the same time. Even with the lights in the parking lot, Joe couldn't see through the SUV's tinted windows.

As he drove, Joe couldn't shake the idea that the SUV was following him. He checked his rearview mirror frequently. Once in a while he'd lose sight of the SUV—but then he'd check again, and there it would be. It seemed to vanish and then materialize like a phantom.

At last Joe reached the hotel. As he pulled into the hotel parking garage, Joe checked his rearview mirror again. Like a scene in a movie, the mirror captured the image of the SUV slowing down as if to turn in after him. Then it sped away.

Joe wheeled the van around in a big U-turn in the parking garage and sped back out onto the street. He could see the SUV a few cars ahead. Carefully, he stayed back, always keeping his target in sight. When he realized they were driving out of town, he opened a map on the passenger seat.

By periodically checking the map and following the signs along the streets and highway, Joe guessed they were driving out to Falcon Lake. On the map the lake appeared as a large body of water in a heavily wooded area west of town. Signs identified the area surrounding the northern half of the lake as a wildlife preserve.

The SUV driver pulled into a secluded area along the road on the north end of the lake and parked the vehicle. Joe followed suit, pulling into a wooded area off the road and out of sight of the SUV driver.

The night was very dark. Only a sliver of a moon shone in the sky.

Ahead of Joe stood a huge shagbark hickory tree with three knots on its trunk. As Joe passed by the tree, the "knots" sprang away from the trunk and fluttered off to join their bat brothers who were busy feasting on mosquitoes and gnats. Lightning bugs glowed and swooped near Joe's head. And what looked like two fireflies in a tree turned out to be the glowing yellow eyes of an owl looking for a midnight snack.

Countless other animals scuttled through the fallen leaves, snapping twigs beneath them. Joe tried to ignore the creepy noises of the dark woods and focus on tracking the person ahead.

Although the woods did not thin out any as Joe went deeper into the preserve, a fresh new scent filled his nose. The ground began sloping down an embankment, and he thought he heard the rhythm of moving water. He hid behind a tree as he and the person he was following neared a small clearing.

As his eyes adjusted to the moonlit scene ahead, he looked around. The ground curved back up again to a spectacular steel-and-glass mansion. It arched above the lake and was surrounded by tall lush trees. A few smaller buildings rose farther back in the woods behind it.

The SUV driver hurried up to the huge house and disappeared around the back. Joe waited a few minutes but saw no more activity around the house. He carefully crept out from behind the tree trunk and started toward the mansion.

He was sure the house would be protected by an alarm system, so he took a moment to scan the branches around the buildings. Though he saw no telltale sign of a security system, he stayed on high alert.

Despite how carefully he was moving, he couldn't shake a weird stabbing sensation in his gut. He felt like every step brought him closer to the house— and farther from safety.

He was only a few yards away when his premonition proved accurate. First floodlights from three different directions pinned him like a wild animal in headlights. Then, with a sound eruption that sent the birds and animals fleeing, a crazy choir of sirens and alarms told the world that Joe was there.

8 Flipped Out

Joe was stunned for a few seconds by the noise and bright lights. When he saw a video camera mounted on the side of the house and aimed right at him, though, he charged into action.

Shielding his face, he raced away from the house and into the dense woods. From behind him he heard a door slam and the pounding of footsteps. In response, Joe ran faster, sprinting through the woods at top speed.

After several minutes he stopped and ducked into a tangle of undergrowth. For a while he heard someone thrashing through the woods. He was sure the person was searching for him.

Eventually it was quiet. He waited a few minutes

to be sure no one was around, then he stepped out from his screen of tangled bushes. Convinced that he was safe, he wound his way back through the trees to the road.

When he reached the secluded area where the SUV was hidden, he stopped. He strained to hear any noise that would indicate he was being followed, but there was nothing but the weird crackles and chirps of the woods at night.

"Okay," Joe whispered. "Let's see what we've got here." He picked the lock of the SUV and quietly opened the passenger door. The inside of the vehicle was totally clean—there was nothing on the seats or floor. He flipped down the visors but found nothing but a mirror attached to the back of one.

Frustrated, he popped open the glove compartment. "That's what I figured," he whispered. "It's a rental—no identification of the driver." He brushed his hands under the driver's seat. One of his fingers trailed across something that felt like a thin rope. He grabbed it and pulled out a short gray cord wrapped around a small bulky roll of black cloth.

This looks familiar, he thought. Joe recognized it as a match to the piece of gray cord Frank had found earlier in their hotel room.

He laid the small bulky package on the front seat of the van and pulled the gray cord. The bundle unrolled, revealing a small tool kit. Inside he found a pair of needlenose pliers, a couple of screwdrivers and small wrenches, a file, a lockpick, and a slim pair of razor-sharp scissors.

He took all the tools out and checked the bottoms of the pockets. They were all empty. There was nothing in the SUV that gave him a clue about the driver's identity.

Joe replaced the tool kit and climbed out of the vehicle. He closed and locked the door, then he raced back to his own van and drove out of the area.

By the time Joe got to the Hardys' hotel room, Frank was in deep sleep. *Better not wake him,* Joe thought. *He's got to be in great shape for the race tomorrow.*

Joe's night was not so peaceful. He spent restless hours reliving his attack outside Hugh Conney's garage and the subsequent pursuit of the SUV driver. Was someone prowling around inside The Rabbit's garage? Was it the same person who grabbed him from behind and nearly choked him? And was there a connection between that person and the driver of the SUV?

Thursday morning Joe woke up to find a note from Frank saying that he'd left for breakfast with the other cyclists.

Joe called J. J.'s cell phone and got voicemail. He left a message saying he was sorry they hadn't connected the previous night, then he suggested that they meet up later that day. Next Joe called Noah and arranged to meet him for breakfast at a café at the track.

Over sausage and Belgian waffles, Joe and Noah talked about the press briefing the night before. "Man, I can't believe it," Joe said. "I wonder how Becky's taking all of this."

"Not very well, I'm sure," Noah answered.

Joe stabbed a piece of sausage. "I hear there's some interesting recreational areas around town," he said casually, changing the subject. He decided not to go into any details about his adventure the night before. "Are there any places to wind-surf or boat?"

"Falcon Lake is pretty cool," Noah said. "It's a wildlife preserve west of town. Nice lake, lots of animals and birds. It's a great place for hiking and water sports."

"That's all public land?" Joe prompted.

"No. The preserve itself is public—it belongs to the city. But it borders only the northern half of the lake. The southern half is surrounded by private property."

"Does all that property belong to one owner?" Joe asked.

"No—actually it's only partially developed," Noah answered, pouring more syrup on his waffle.

"Some of the land is still as raw as the preserve. The rest is divided into a few very secluded, very exclusive estates. All of the land *has* been sold. The undeveloped part will be developed eventually."

"Who owns the estates?" Joe asked.

"Most are owned by local industrialists," Noah answered. "They use them for entertaining or as guest houses for clients or friends who travel here from abroad. I'm sure we've got Grand Prix fans staying in some of them this week." Noah sipped his coffee. "And a few of the homes are owned by local sports celebrities," he continued. "You know—pro basketball and football players. Some of them might be at the party for the burn center on Friday night, by the way. It's a good opportunity to interview celebrities from other sports."

Joe and Noah finished their food and paid their bills. Outside, the sun was shooting through red and gold leaves. The air was warm but crisp with the scent of autumn.

"It's a great day for Frank's race," Noah said as they walked toward the parking lot. "I think I'll head on over now and get a feature or two for the evening news. You want to ride with me?"

"No, thanks. I need to do a little work before the race," Joe said. "I have about an hour. I'll be over in a little while. J. J.'s planning to go too. Save us some seats?"

"You got it," Noah said. He quickly got into his car and drove off.

Joe climbed into the back of the Hardys' van, closed the door, and fired up his laptop computer. Armed with the information Noah had given him, he went to the Internet. It took him only a few clicks to access the county's office of land records.

Within moments Joe had zoomed in on the fifteen-acre property where he'd been with the SUV driver the night before. Then, using the code number for the property, he matched it to the list of landowners at Falcon Lake.

"ManxInc.," he read aloud, jotting the name of the owner of the specific estate he was at down on a notepad.

Joe closed out that site and then typed the name he'd just written in the Search box on the screen. Nothing came up. He tried a few other variations of the name to start a search, but he didn't find anything. He finally gave up and shut down his computer. Tucking the note in his pocket, he drove out of the media center's parking lot.

Close to the Velodrome, Frank shared breakfast with the other cyclists in the race. A local restaurant had provided the carbo-rich meal. Frank filled up on pasta and vegetables.

After breakfast a shuttle took Frank and the other

racers the few miles to the Major Taylor Velodrome. Frank grabbed his bike and his gym bag and checked in to get his starting number. Then he peeled off his sweats and took a few minutes to do some warm-up exercises in his racing shorts and shirt.

The bikers were allowed a half hour for practice runs around the track. Frank pulled on his numbered racing jersey and walked his bike onto the track to join the others. After a few loops of the track, his left pedal felt a little loose, so he pulled off to make an adjustment. Then he wheeled back out onto the track. The bike felt great as he finished his practice.

As he waited for the countdown, Frank glanced around the small open stadium and up into the stands. He saw Joe and J. J. sitting together, and smiled as Joe let loose with a shrill whistle. In the far corner, he saw Noah and Becky talking to a couple of television sports reporters.

At last the race began. Frank hit the track with a great start. All the ache from his bruising bellyflop the day before seemed to disappear as he cranked the bike up to top speed. The pedal was tight and became one unit with his foot. He felt a familiar rush of adrenaline flood through him as he rode, and his mind cleared to concentrate only on the task at hand.

He picked up speed, masterfully maneuvering his bike around the other bikers. He smoothly changed lanes from the long outside one to the shorter inside path. As he flew around the track, he felt totally pumped.

His knees wobbled first. As he drew them up, the front wheel seemed to give. And then, without warning, his bike seemed to fly apart. The last thing he saw was the guardrail rushing toward him.

9 Where There's Smoke . . .

Frank barreled into the rail like a cannonball. He then slid along the top for a few feet before landing in a crumpled heap back on the track. Every part of his body seemed numb except the front of his left leg. From the knee down it felt as if someone were roasting it in a bonfire.

He sat up slowly and looked down at his leg. His entire shin was scraped. His lower leg seemed to swell as he watched.

A race official and the doctor on call hurried over to Frank. "We'd better get a gurney," the doctor said, motioning for a stretcher.

"No," Frank said. "I'm okay. I can walk." He stood up and put his foot down. The pain from his leg radiated up into his brain, and he could feel his face contort into a grimace.

The race slowed when Frank crashed. Cyclists held their positions and slowly circled the track.

The two men who'd hurried over propped Frank up and helped him hop off the track. Spectators clapped as he made his way to the exit. He nodded and smiled at the crowd as he left the track on his human crutches.

Joe was waiting for them at the door to the medical examining room. "Man, that is one nasty-looking leg," he said. "How do you feel?"

"I've been better," Frank said with a laugh. "A *lot* better."

"Hey, Frank," J. J. called out. He was joined by Noah and Becky. Noah held one of Frank's bike wheels in his hand. They stayed in the hall as the doctor and Joe helped Frank into the examining room and up onto the table. The doctor took nearly a half an hour to clean, medicate, and dress the foot-long scrape. Then he gave Frank a tube of antibiotic medicine, which had a topical anesthetic in it to help dull the pain. He also gave him gauze and tape so that Frank could change the dressings himself.

By the time the doctor finished, Frank's pain had subsided. He and Joe went out into the hall. J. J., Becky, and Noah were still there. They all seemed relieved to see Frank limp on his own.

"The equipment squad brought your bike down," J. J. said, his forehead wrinkled with concern. "What's left of it, that is."

Frank looked at the pile of bike pieces and felt like he'd been punched. His prized bike—the one that had taken him to a couple of finish lines in first place—was totaled!

He and Joe carefully packed the pieces of the bike up in boxes provided by the equipment squad. "The race should be over soon," Frank said, lifting one of the bike's wheels into the box. "Afterward I want to do a thorough search of the track—and make sure there are no more parts out there."

As Joe and J. J. brought the boxes outside, Frank, Noah, and Becky headed back to the track. "Do you guys have any idea what happened?" Noah asked. "I saw you making some adjustments during the practice, Frank."

"It was really weird," Becky noted. "The bike just seemed to fly apart."

"That's the way *I* felt too," Frank said, trying to remember the moments leading up to his crash. "I don't really know what happened—but you can *bet* I'm going to find out."

The cyclists were racing in full force by the time Frank and the others got back to the track. Joe and J. J. soon joined them, and they all sat on the benches and cheered the other cyclists on.

After the race, J. J., Noah, and Becky took off. The Hardys stayed at the Velodrome, though, and combed the area for fragments of Frank's bike. Joe found a seat spring and a steering pin; Frank found a couple of bolts. They added these last parts to the boxes in the van, and Joe drove them back to the hotel.

"I'll be okay once I get cleaned up," Frank said as they entered their room. "You know, we were supposed to get together with Becky after the race. But there was so much going on, I didn't get a chance to talk to her. We need to get on that."

Joe noticed the red light flashing on the phone next to his bed. "We got a message." He called the hotel switchboard and listened to the voicemail. "Becky called," he said, hanging up. "She asked us to meet her at four-thirty at the paddock entrance."

Frank checked his watch. "We can do that," he said. "She says she has evidence for us."

"Plus we need to find out more about this Doobie Poliano guy and whether he's really been seen around here or not," Joe added.

"And now we also have to ask Becky about Hugh's arrest," Frank added. "That's got to be a blow."

"First, though, you and I have to talk," Joe said. "I ran into some trouble myself last night."

"Okay," Frank said. "Let me peel off my racing clothes and get cleaned up, and then we'll talk."

Frank washed up and changed into jeans and a sweater. When he finished, he found a tray full of burgers, fries, and shakes waiting. "I ordered room service," Joe said, grinning.

"Great idea," Frank said, grabbing a burger. "We totally missed lunch."

In between bites, Joe told Frank about his attack the night before, outside The Rabbit's garage.

"What did this person look like?" Frank asked.

"Black jeans, dark green jacket, and a pointed knit cap pulled down so I couldn't see his face," Joe said.

"That sounds like it could be the guy who broke into our room earlier," Frank said.

"Wait—the story gets better," Joe said. He told his brother about being followed by the SUV, and then about trading places and following the SUV himself. Then he described the estate at Falcon Lake.

"But here's the best part," Joe said, homing in on the end of his story. He told Frank about getting into the SUV. "It was a rental, so I didn't find any identification. But there was something interesting under the driver's seat." He described the tool kit with the gray tie.

Frank went to his sports bag and took out the gray cord he'd found on the desk earlier. "It looked like this?" he asked.

"*Exactly* like that," Joe said. "In fact the end of the cord was even a little frayed like that one. I figure the toolkit had two pieces of cord that tied together to hold the bundle closed. This one must have fallen off."

Frank nodded. "I'd like to get my hands on that tool kit and compare the two cords."

Joe told Frank about talking with Noah about who owned the estates on Falcon Lake. "I checked the Internet and the owner for the property I was on is ManxInc. I searched for information about that exact name and variations of it, but came up with nothing—so far."

"Do we figure that the guy who followed you in the SUV is the same one who tried to strangle you outside Hugh Conney's garage?"

"Probably. Don't you think?" Joe asked.

"Yeah, probably," Frank repeated. He started pacing. "This case is all about 'probably,' though. We've got a lot of stuff happening, several suspects, and *no* concrete evidence to prove any of it. We don't even have real proof that the crimes actually happened. Sometimes I wonder if we even have a real case here."

"I think we do," Joe said. "I may have found something that falls into the real evidence category. And you're not going to like it."

Joe laid out a handful of bolts on the desk. Then he took a small leather envelope the size of a credit card from his wallet. From the inside of the envelope, he pulled a paper-thin rectangle of magnifying glass and handed it to Frank. "I checked over what's left of your bike while you were cleaning up," he said. "Take a look."

Frank picked up each piece and turned it over and around, examining it carefully through the magnifier. He felt a rippling chill, as if a sliver of ice was sliding down his back. He quickly looked at Joe.

"These were brand new bolts before I started today," Frank said.

"And the threads are now nearly stripped," Joe added. "They've been filed down—not enough to keep you from starting the race—"

"But more than enough to keep me from finishing it." Images flashed through Frank's mind like movie previews: the loose pedal, the wobbly front wheel, his body slamming into the guard rail. Then he focused on one image: the intruder backing out of their hotel room. "Are we thinking the same thing here?" he asked his brother.

"The guy breaks in here with a tool kit, files your bolts, reassembles the bike . . . "

"And it could be the same person who followed you and drove the SUV to Falcon Lake," Frank said.

"We have to find him—or her," Frank said. "It looks like we have a real case after all, and these bolts could be a major clue. There's no reason to attack us unless this person is trying to scare us away from the truth."

"We must be closer to it than we thought," Joe pointed out, "and this guy knows it."

"If we find him, we find the tool kit," Frank said. "Then we'll check the pocket that the file is in. Chances are there will be filing grit that will match what's left of these bolts."

"Okay, where do we start?" Joe asked.

"Falcon Lake," the Hardys said in unison.

They checked their sports bags, making sure they had the gear they figured they might need: flashlights, lockpicks, penknives, small empty containers, and a mini camera.

"First, though, we need to meet with Becky," Frank said, checking his watch.

The Hardys arrived at the track at about four-fifteen and headed straight for the paddock. "If we see J. J.," Joe said as they walked, "one of us needs to talk to him. He has some information about the drinking bottle from Manion's car."

"Okay, let's watch for him," Frank agreed. "If he shows up, I'll get together with him, and you can talk to Becky. And neither one is to know about the other meeting, okay?"

"Right. And let's be sure to ask each of them about Doobie Poliano," Joe added. "Is he in town, and if so, why? Hey, speaking of J. J., there he is." Joe nodded toward the track medical center. J. J. was going inside the building.

"I'm on it," Frank said. "Let me have the swipe card he gave us? You go meet Becky. I'll get the information from J. J. and then use the swipe card to get into the paddock. I'll meet you at The Rabbit's garage after I've finished talking to J. J."

As Frank veered off to the medical center, Joe continued to the paddock. Becky was waiting for him. She was clearly very upset and distracted as they walked to Hugh Conney's garage.

"I didn't really get a chance to talk to you at the bike race this morning," Joe said. "Hugh's arrest must have been a real blow."

"It's absurd," Becky said. "Hugh was trying to help Manion—and look where it got him. You've got to help me show the world the truth. No one's in here right now, so this will be a good place to talk."

She took out her keys to open the door, and Joe felt a shock of recognition zap through his chest. "Hey, where did you get that?" he asked Becky as they stepped inside.

She locked the door behind them, the same way J. J. had when he'd taken the Hardys into Manion's garage. The light was dim inside. Joe looked at the blackened window and flashed on his attack outside.

"What?" Becky asked, looking in her hand. "You

mean this?" She held up the silver metal triangle that had been strung on her key ring. It matched the one Frank had found in the hotel stairwell, except the number was 23 instead of 17.

"Yes," Joe said. "What is it exactly?"

"I don't know," Becky said. "It came with the keys. I think it has something to do with the Grand Prix in Monza—a garage number or a qualifying number. Something like that. Why?"

"Can you find out?" Joe asked. "Find out exactly where it came from and what it means."

"Sure," Becky said, dropping the keys back in her pocket. She hoisted her bag onto a worktable and began fishing through it. As she turned on a bright light in the room, Joe heard strange sounds: first a sort of whirring noise, and then scraping and creaking.

He turned quickly to locate the sounds. They came from the window. As he watched, the window inched open. A white rag dropped through and hit the floor. Then the window slowly closed, and Joe heard the whirring again.

Joe's throat felt suddenly parched, as if all the liquid had drained from it. His eyes burned as he watched the rag disappear into a clump of powder. Then, with a loud whooooosh, a jacket hanging on the back of a nearby chair started to disappear. It was as if it were being eaten by invisible bugs.

All this happened in just a few seconds—and that's all it took for Joe to realize what was going on. The rag had brought a deadly intruder.

"Becky!" he shouted. "Fire! Get out—*now!*"

Joe didn't wait for her to understand. He grabbed her hand and streaked to the door. As he fumbled with the lock, he could feel the heat spreading toward them.

10 Playing with All the Marbles

Joe opened the door slightly and pushed Becky through. He then grabbed the extinguisher hanging by the door, turned it toward the room, and sprayed the fire as he backed out the door himself. He heard Becky yelling for the fire crew.

Firemen quickly arrived at the scene. Joe ran around to the window at the back of the building. He crouched to look at the ground as he searched his memory for the moment when he first heard noises outside the window.

"Hey, you okay?" Frank asked, running up to join Joe.

"Yeah," Joe answered.

"Becky said someone dropped a rag burning with

race car fuel in the window," Frank said. "The fire chief's launched an arson investigation."

"Well, they need to see this," Joe said, pointing to the ground. "I heard a whirring noise just before the window opened and after it closed. It was a power scooter. Some of the drivers use them to get around the track."

Frank crouched next to his brother. "I see what you mean. There's a fresh track right there."

"And a footprint next to it," Joe pointed out.

A few minutes later Joe and Becky gave their statements to the firemen as well as the police, who had arrived.

"Well, that's about all we can do for now, I guess," Becky said after the officers left. She sounded worn out. "With Hugh's arrest, though, and now this . . . our Grand Prix season is over. And Manion wins."

"Let's get something to drink," Joe suggested, temporarily changing the subject. "My throat feels like sandpaper after being exposed to that fire."

"Okay," Becky said, "but let's go somewhere far away from the garages and the smell of that burning fuel." Joe and Becky walked several yards until they found a table under a scarlet maple tree. Frank went to a kiosk and got some slushy fruit drinks. When he returned, Becky was in tears.

Frank handed her a drink. "Look, I know how you

must feel," he said gently. "Joe and I are determined to get to the bottom of this. You told us that you had a parts shipment stolen, a falsified scrutineering report, and a gauge that someone altered to a dangerous setting."

"Right," Becky said.

"Have there been any more developments in the investigations of those incidents?"

"No," Becky admitted. "The parts were never tracked down. The scrutineering report was straightened out, and our mechanics found the altered gauge and fixed that. Hugh received a couple of threatening phone calls, too, but they couldn't be traced. By the way, how's your leg?"

"It's feeling better, thanks," Frank answered. "What's the story on Hugh's arrest?"

"It's completely bogus," Becky said.

"Before the fire, you said he was just trying to help Manion," Joe said. "What did you mean?"

"Hugh admits that he and Manion had an argument under the stands," Becky said. "But there was no real fight. At one point, Manion collapsed. He'd left the hospital before the doctors wanted him to. Hugh picked him up to take him back to the medical center. Manion got his strength back, though, wrestled free, and took off. Hugh doesn't know where he went. We figure he's hiding somewhere."

"The police said an eyewitness saw the argument, and there was a lot of shoving," Frank said. "The witness saw Hugh carry Manion off, then tried to get closer for a better view and missed what happened after that. Who's the witness?"

"Not sure," Becky said. "But rumor has it that it's Bill Katt."

"Okay, we'll check with him," Frank said.

"Show Frank your keys," Joe asked her.

Becky got out her key ring and laid it on the table. Frank zeroed in on the silver triangle. "Where did this come from?" he asked.

"I told Joe I'm not sure," Becky answered. "These are the paddock keys—Brian, our team owner, gave them to me. I'll find out what it is. I told Joe that I think it has something to do with the Monza Grand Prix." She reached in her bag. "Meanwhile, check into this guy." She handed Frank a file on Doobie Poliano.

"Noah said you'd seen him here in Indy," Joe told her. "Where was that?"

"Well, I didn't actually see him," Becky said.

"Who has?" Joe asked.

"Some of Hugh's mechanics," she answered. "Look, I'm not playing games with you guys. I'm just trying to prove that Hugh isn't guilty of anything. Doobie definitely could be targeting Manion—and setting up Hugh to catch the blame. Just look over the file. You'll see what I mean."

"Has anyone mentioned this to the police?" Joe asked.

"Yes. Brian, our team owner, told the local police and the track security about it. But he still believes Manion's the one behind it all." Becky took another slurp of her fruit slush. "I'd better get back to the suite," she said. "Everyone will have heard about the fire by now. I'll have to get out a press release. Thanks again for helping, guys. I know you'll prove Hugh's innocence."

She turned to Joe. "And you," she said, "you saved my life. I wish I could repay you somehow." She smiled. "Hey, I've got it. How about a spin in the backup car?"

"You're kidding!" Joe said. "Me, drive a Formula One car? When?"

"It will have to be late, when no one else is around. And it will have to be tonight. Tomorrow night is the charity party for the burn center. Saturday night is out because of the race Sunday."

She smiled at Joe. "So how about tonight? My whole team will be downtown with lawyers or prosecutors. The other teams will be asleep, getting rest before official practice tomorrow. There'll be some night security people around, but I can handle them. Meet me at the garage at two o'clock. Here's a swipe card to get you in."

She handed Joe a card like the one J. J. had given Joe, then left.

"Where do you think Manion is?" Frank asked as they watched Becky walk off.

"There are a lot of rumors floating around," Joe said, "but Bill told me he thinks Manion's gone back to Monaco for a little R and R. He's sure he'll show up tomorrow, though, ready to drive."

Frank spread the pages from Becky on the table. There were newspaper articles from around the world, a few Grand Prix programs from ten years ago, and photographs of Doobie Poliano.

"It's like Noah told me," Frank said. "Poliano hired Manion as a rookie. Manion joined Savanne's team. Poliano went bankrupt soon after."

"Here's an interview with him in a London newspaper," Joe said, showing Frank an article. "He blames Manion for his bankruptcy—even says that Manion stole money from him."

"This picture is ten years old," Frank said, holding up a black-and-white glossy photo. "He could be the one I trapped in the stairwell."

"I didn't see the driver of the SUV because the windows were tinted. But he could be the guy that tried to strangle me earlier outside The Rabbit's garage," Joe agreed. "He might even have been casing the place to set the fire."

"We've got attacks against Manion, and Hugh is implicated," Frank said. "Then problems for Hugh, and Manion looks guilty. Either way, Manion loses."

"So Doobie Poliano could be behind all this stuff, right?" Joe asked.

"Maybe these crimes aren't what they seem,"

Frank said. "Maybe J. J. and Becky are both right and neither driver is to blame. Doobie might be setting up both, framing Manion for revenge and framing Hugh to get Manion into further trouble."

"I say we go to Falcon Lake," Joe said.

It didn't take long for Frank and Joe to get in the van and drive west of town into the secluded pull-off near the lake. "The house was on a hill, above a cove," Joe told Frank. He pointed to the spot on the map of the lake. "I say we go by boat. We can pull up here." He drew a circle on a curve of the bank. "It'll be out of sight from anyone at the estate."

"The map says we can rent a boat in the wildlife preserve," Frank said.

The Hardys walked to the preserve's boathouse, picked a canoe, and paddled off from the northern part of the lake. The sun had gone down, but there was still a rosy gold glow coming from the sky.

"There it is," Joe said, his voice hushed. From the water, they saw the huge house perched on a hill. Everything was very quiet. Only a few birds were calling.

The Hardys hid the canoe and climbed to the woods around the estate. Frank's leg was still a little sore, but not enough to keep him from climbing the hill.

There was no sign of anyone else near the estate. "The alarms you tripped last night were probably motion alarms," Frank whispered. "They're harder to see."

"Yep," Joe agreed. "Let's watch for them."

As they circled the mansion they found several alarms. Each time, Joe used tools from his bag to disarm the device. Finally they felt that it was safe for them to search the outbuildings at the edge of the woods. Two garages, a garden house, a tool shed, a pool house, and a log cabin were all empty. "This is weird," Joe whispered.

By the time they circled the property, it was eight o'clock. The rosy cast had left the sky, and a navy blue darkness began to cloak the horizon. Cautiously, the teens crept to the main house. The windows were mostly shielded by curtains, but they could see around the edges.

"The place looks empty," Frank said. He shone a small penlight through the edge of the window. "There's nothing in there—no furniture, no people. Nothing."

"We can't see what's happening on the upper floors from here," Joe said. "I'll be right back."

Joe took Frank's penlight and scrambled up a heavy wooden trellis that was attached to the house. Quickly he ran across a balcony, shining his light along the edge of the windows. He climbed up a drainspout to the top floor and checked the windows at that level.

In a short time, he was back on the ground.

"Nothing," he reported. "The place is empty." He wiped his forehead. "It's starting to rain."

"Okay, let's get out of here," Frank said. The Hardys retraced their steps to the canoe and paddled back to the boathouse. Then they hurried to the van and drove back to town. It wasn't really raining yet—just drizzling.

"It's almost midnight," Frank said. "I need to file my story about Hugh's arrest. Let's go to the media center. We can stay there until it's time to meet Becky."

The Hardys picked up sandwiches, drove to the media center, and got to work. After an hour, Joe broke the silence.

"I can't wait any longer," Joe said. "It's one o'clock. Becky's probably there. Let's go! I'm afraid she'll cancel if the rain kicks up a notch."

The teens found Becky alone inside the garage. She looked worried when they first walked in, but her face brightened up when she saw who they were. "Ready to drive?" she asked Joe.

"Oh, man, I am *so* ready," Joe answered.

"I have to tell you that if it's really raining out there, we're going to have to postpone," Becky said. "I've checked you out and I know you actually did ride in an Indy 500 car, so I trust you. And Formula One races go on regardless of rain, so the cars can take it. But if it gets bad, I'm pulling you in."

"I hear you," Joe said. "Let's go."

100

Becky helped him into the driver's suit. "Everything's fireproof from top to bottom," Becky said, "but don't feel you have to test it." She handed him a helmet. "These are called trip strips," she said, pointing to wings on both sides of the helmet. "These keep your head stable—you can get up to six Gs when you decelerate! There are also vent holes for air, an earphone, and a microphone." She ticked off various features. "You know what marbles are, right?" she asked. "The bits of debris and tire pieces that clog the track." Joe nodded. "If your visor gets gritty or smacked up with marbles," she concluded, "you can peel off layers of it, one at a time."

Joe put on the helmet. When he pulled down the visor his entire head was covered down to his neck. He slid down into the car and fastened the harness.

Becky pointed out a few of the cockpit features. "You can change gears without your hands leaving the steering wheel." She showed him the two paddles behind the wheel. "Flick the right paddle to go up a gear, the left to go down."

She continued pointing out over two dozen buttons, levers, and digital displays in the cockpit. "And don't forget—Formula One tires are no longer slick like the Indy tires. Are you ready?"

Joe gave her the thumbs-up sign. Frank and Becky pulled on rain parkas and pushed the car out of the garage, along the pit road, and onto the track.

Joe gave Frank and Becky the thumbs-up sign again. Then he started the engine.

Joe eased the car up to one hundred miles per hour, then one twenty, then one fifty. He followed the groove and whipped into a curve.

There were a few wet spots on the track. He maneuvered around them without much trouble. He was swinging onto a short straightaway when he saw what looked like a mirage up ahead. A shadow seemed to form in the dark of curve four. It got bigger as he zoomed closer. It was like a ghost, swaying in the mist.

"What *is* that?" Joe was startled by the sound of his own voice, muffled through his helmet. *"I don't believe it,* he told himself. *It's a person. Someone's standing on the track.*

"Get off!" he yelled instinctively, even though he knew the scream of the engine would drown out his cries. "Get off the track!"

He decelerated and veered to the left. He saw the small puddle too late. He felt the car lose contact with the track and shoot forward into the air. The last thing he saw as he launched into the air was Manion Cristal's face.

11 A Sinister Sip

Joe felt the pressure in his knees and feet as he worked the brakes—even though brakes wouldn't help him as he sailed through the air.

The car came back to earth with a thud, right-side up. He felt the landing in his seat, and then a jamming shock up his spine and into his skull. He undid the harness and pulled himself out of the cockpit. Frank and Becky arrived immediately in her team's small tow truck.

"Man, that was incredible," Joe said, shaking his head to get rid of the ringing he heard in his brain. "You won't believe what—"

"Are you okay?" Becky cried as she ran up.

"What happened?" Frank asked. "Did you run into a puddle?"

"That's what I'm trying to tell you," Joe said. "There was someone on the track—and I think it was Manion!"

Joe started running across the infield, back toward curve four. He could hear Frank running behind him and the tow truck starting up. Because Frank and Joe took a shortcut, they beat Becky in the truck.

"Whoa, you're right," Frank said when they reached the spot where Joe had left the track. There, standing in the middle of the groove, was Manion Cristal.

"Manion! What on earth are you doing out here?" Becky called out as she drove up.

"That isn't your business. The question is why are you"—he turned to Joe—"trying to kill me?"

"Hold it, man," Joe said, holding his arms up to deflect the blow from Manion's swinging arms.

"Don't tell me. You're walking the course, right?" Becky asked.

"You know I always do that the night before the track officially opens," Manion answered, dropping his arms in a huff. "I always walk the full race through once. It helps me get psyched for practice and qualifications."

"Where have you been?" Frank asked the driver. "Everyone's been looking for you."

"I flew my plane home," Manion answered, "to Monte Carlo. I rested in my villa and ate my mother's food. Now I am all healed and ready to claim the Formula One championship!"

He turned to continue walking, but he quickly wheeled around again. "I make you a bargain," he said. "You do not tell anyone you have seen *me* here tonight, and I will not tell anyone I have seen *you* here tonight. Tomorrow morning, I will make my own announcement." He walked on along the track.

Frank, Joe, and Becky rode back to the backup car, hooked it to the back of the mini tow truck, and pulled it back to the garage.

"That was sensational," Joe told Becky as the three prepared to leave the paddock. "I'll never forget it—even if I didn't drive the whole circuit."

"Great," Becky said. "You earned it. Just don't ever tell anyone!"

"You got it," Joe answered.

"And we're keeping quiet about Manion, right?" Frank said.

"Looks like we have to," Becky answered, "or he'll tell everyone you drove tonight."

"Everyone will know he's back by tomorrow morning anyway," Frank reminded her. "He'll be at the track opening."

"I know," Becky answered. "Oh, I almost forgot. You asked about this silver triangle on my keyring?" She held it up. "Well, it's a garage tag, like I thought. Only it isn't from Monza. It's from the Melbourne Grand Prix ten years ago. Everyone who was there got these with their garage keys. Apparently they only gave these out for a couple of years. Now they use combination locks. Brian always puts this old one on the garage keys for luck, because the year he got this, Hugh won his first race."

The Hardys wished Becky a good night—what was left of it—and drove back to the hotel. "Man, I'm totally beat," Frank said. He didn't mention it, but his leg was throbbing with a dull ache.

"With Manion back, the race really heats up again," Joe said, dropping his bag at the foot of his bed. He sat down and pulled off his cross-trainers. "I still can't believe I drove that track."

Frank smiled at his brother, then he became very serious. "We need to keep everything tight from now on," he said. "Just between us. We don't tell Noah or J. J. or Becky what we're thinking."

"Okay, but why the secrecy?"

"If we're right, and Doobie Poliano attacked us both, he has to know we're investigating all the incidents around the track."

"Which means he must be behind them," Joe said. "Otherwise he wouldn't be trying to shut us down."

"True, but that's not my point. My question is, how would he know we're on the case? One of those three—Noah, J. J., or Becky—would have told him. It might have been an accident or a slip of the tongue. But nevertheless, it's pretty clear to me that he knows. So from now on, we keep quiet."

While he talked, Frank cleaned his leg wound and changed the dressing.

"Speaking of J. J., what did you find out when you tracked him down at the medical center?"

"I was just getting to that," Frank answered. "He's arranged for us to talk to the pit chief—the head mechanic for his team."

"Those mechanics haven't been too friendly so far," Joe said. "They totally turn off when I ask them any questions."

"J. J. said he fixed that, and he's pretty sure they'll trust us now. We can meet with him before breakfast tomorrow, at seven-thirty."

"That's just a few hours from now," Joe groaned, pulling the covers over his head.

Frank could hardly believe how good it felt to rest his leg on the bed. "I've got a plan," he whispered before falling asleep.

By Friday morning, the previous night's drizzle was just a memory. The sun streamed brightly through the autumn leaves, and the temperature was rising back up into the seventies. It was a perfect day for the official opening of the U.S. Grand Prix.

Frank's leg felt tight and a little stiff, but it wasn't nearly as sore as it had been the night before. The Hardys had awakened at six-forty-five, and were showered, dressed, and in the van by seven-fifteen.

"We've got a lot to do today," Joe said. "The track

opens to the public at nine this morning, and that's when the teams hit the track for practice. With Manion back, the danger quotient is back up."

"Hugh will be back in his car too," Frank pointed out. "Now that Manion has returned, they've got no reason to hold Hugh as a material witness in his disappearance anymore."

"We've got to make some headway on this case," Joe said. "The closer we get to the race on Sunday, the more dangerous this thing becomes."

"Okay," Frank said, "we've got a lot of questions. Is Doobie Poliano really in town? If so, where is he? Is he the one that followed you home and the one whom you followed out to Falcon Lake? Why was he going out there?"

"Did he break into our room and sabotage your bike?" Joe added. "And did he have anything to do with the fire in The Rabbit's garage?"

"How about this? We split up this morning," Frank said. "We've both got swipe cards now, so we'll each have full access to everything. I'll talk to J. J.'s pit chief and find out what happened to the drinking bottle after Manion's crash. Then I'll try to find out who had garage seventeen at the Melbourne Grand Prix. And I'll check with hotel security again and see if they know anything more about the break-in."

"I'll try to track down Becky and see how the arson investigation is going," Joe offered. "And I'll also see if I can track down Doobie Poliano. Becky said some of Hugh's mechanics saw him in town. I'll also find out more about ManxInc., the company that owns the estate on Falcon Lake."

Joe pulled the van into the media parking lot. "If we don't happen to meet up before noon, I'll meet you then at the media center, okay?"

"Good plan," Frank said.

Nearly a quarter of a million fans were already in place, ready to see the first real practice of the weekend. Large colorful banners waved in the breeze, and airhorns, loudspeakers, and revving engines filled the air with sound.

The Hardys gobbled down breakfast sandwiches, then sped straight to the paddock. Joe headed for The Rabbit's garage, and Frank turned toward Manion's.

J. J. was waiting for the elder Hardy. "Hey, Frank, I'm glad you made it. How's the leg?"

"It's okay," Frank said. "Your team all ready for practice this morning?"

"I guess you heard that Manion's back. He flew home to rest up, and he's back up to full strength now."

"Yeah, I heard." *Looks like Manion kept his word about seeing us last night,* Frank thought with relief. "So, is your mechanic ready to talk to me?"

"He's inside," J. J. said, "in the office in the back corner of the garage. Don't keep him long. We need him in the pits."

"No problem," Frank assured J. J. as he walked to the building. A couple of men were getting ready to push Manion's car out to the track. Manion and Kristièn were talking quietly near a worktable. Frank nodded at them and walked to the open door in the back corner. A young man with silvery hair sat waiting behind a desk.

"Hi, I'm Frank Hardy," Frank said, taking the chair next to the desk. "Thanks for taking time to talk to me. This won't take long."

"I appreciate that," the man said in a French accent. "I'm Jacques Herman. J. J. says you want to talk about the drinking bottle in Manion's car."

"I do," Frank said. "Was the drinking bottle still in the cockpit when the car was towed back after Manion's crash?"

"Yes. But it was taken out and sent to a special laboratory for analysis and investigation."

"What kind of lab?" Frank asked. "Was it a university or hospital, or a commercial lab?"

"It is a chemical research place," Jacques answered. "It specializes in biological and chemical poisons."

"Do you mean Bill Katt's company?" Frank asked.

"That's right," Jacques said. "KattTEK. People in automobile racing are like a fraternity—no, more like a family. We fight and we compete, but when we are in trouble, we keep it within the family. We turn to our own for help."

"So you all think Manion might have been poisoned," Frank said.

"It would not be the first time that Hugh Conney stepped over the line in order to knock us out of the race. We will soon find out the truth."

"We already have it," J. J. said, bursting into the office with a paper in his hand. His face was a purplish color and the anger radiated from his dark eyes. "Here's the report from Katt's lab. Hugh went too far this time!"

12 Rats and Roaches

Frank scanned the papers J. J. had thrown on the desk. A few words leaped off the page: poison . . . disorientation . . . lose consciousness . . . nonfatal . . . lining the tube . . . in the drinking bottle.

"Hugh Conney went too far this time," J. J. repeated. "Just a few sips—that's all it took for Manion to black out. Kristièn has already called the police. This time when Hugh is arrested, it will be as a suspect, not a material witness. And it will be for attempted murder!"

Jacques left the office to tell the other mechanics and to help push the car to the track. Frank and J. J. followed him.

"The report says that the poison was nonlethal," J. J. said in a sneering tone. "Knocking out a driver

112

racing a car at two hundred miles an hour, though, is extremely lethal!"

Noah ran up to greet Frank and J. J. "I just heard the news," he said. "Come on, J. J. Tell me exactly what happened."

"Oh, I'll tell you," J. J. said. "You'll get the full story!"

As J. J. began explaining the lab's report, Frank casually backed away. He already had one of the answers he was tracking down. It was time to go after the other two.

While Frank was talking to the mechanic, Joe was talking to two members of Hugh's crew in the pit. Becky had rounded them up and told them to tell Joe everything they knew.

"Where did you see Doobie Poliano here in Indy?" Joe asked, coming right to the point.

"Well, I saw him up in the stands the first time," one of the men said. "He was sitting a couple of rows up from Manion Cristal's pit. He looked about the same as always." The man described Doobie to Joe. The description definitely matched the man Frank had trapped in the hotel stairwell. It also could match the man Joe contended with outside Hugh's garage.

"The only time I saw him was downtown," the other mechanic said. "He was coming out of a dumpy motel near the train station." He wrote down the address and handed it to Joe.

They talked a little more about Doobie's background, but had to stop when it got close to practice time. Joe really wanted to stay and watch, but he pulled himself away.

Joe looked for Frank in the pits, in the paddock, and in the media center, but he couldn't find him. He checked his watch. It was ten-thirty. *Enough time to get downtown and back,* he told himself.

He called Frank's cell phone and left a message. "I got an address for a motel where Doobie has been seen," he said. He gave the address, then continued his message. "It's ten-thirty. If you can get away in the next half hour, join me down there. Otherwise it's back to the original plan and I'll meet you at the media center at noon."

Joe drove into town, then headed south to the address the mechanic had given him. "Hmmm . . . 'dumpy' might have been too nice a word to describe this place," he said. He pulled into the parking lot and went inside. There was no one behind the reservation desk. Joe stood in front of the old computer and punched a few keys. Under the letter P there was no listing for D. B. Poliano. But there *was* a D. Pollen.

That's got to be him, Joe decided. *And he's in room 8.*

"Can I help you?" A man with a mullet strode in and gave Joe a suspicious look.

"I was just waiting to talk about a reservation,"

Joe said quickly. "And I couldn't help but notice your computer. It's almost an antique now. I'm sort of a collector. I haven't seen one of these for a long time."

"It's yours for the right price," the man said. "How's seventy-five dollars?"

"I'll have to talk it over with my partner," Joe said.

"Sure," the motel worker said. "Now when do you want a room? We're getting pretty booked, what with the race and all."

"We were thinking tomorrow night," Joe said. "But I'll get back to you. We might need it longer." He hurried out of the office and back to his van.

When he was sure the reservations clerk wasn't watching, Joe circled behind the van and headed for room 8. It was third from the end of a line of battered doors.

He stood outside the door to room 8 for a moment and listened. He heard no sounds coming from the room—no radio, no water running. He heard nothing that told him someone might be inside. He rapped on the door. No response.

The sudden sound of someone rushing toward him made him jump. Joe stepped away from the door and turned to see who it was.

"I got your message," Frank said, walking up with a smile on his face. In the background, his cab sped away. "I couldn't wait until noon to tell you about Manion's onboard drinking bottle." He filled Joe in on the revelation.

"So he really *was* poisoned," Joe said. "But no one's talking about any *real* proof that The Rabbit or anyone from his team did it?"

"I don't think so," Frank said. "Manion's team would be shouting it to everyone if that were the case." He nodded toward room 8. "Is that his room?"

"Well, it's the room of someone named D. Pollen," Joe said, smirking.

"Close enough," Frank said. "I take it no one's home?"

"No one answered my knock," Joe told him, "And I didn't hear anything from inside." He looked around. "It's an old-fashioned lock, and this place is so beat up it probably doesn't work very well anyway. But we're a little exposed out here in the open."

"Did you go around to the back of the building?" Frank asked. "Maybe there's a window in the bathroom."

"I was headed there when I heard your footsteps. Let's check it out."

The Hardys went around the end of the building and turned the corner. Littered with garbage, the alley at the back of the motel was hidden from the parking lot and any passersby.

Joe counted windows until they reached the third from the end. "This must be it," he whispered. The window was large enough to get his body through, but it was located very high on the wall. With his foot, he slid an overturned wooden crate toward the building. His skin crawled when he heard scratching noises coming from under the crate.

"Stand back," he warned. He stepped back himself and stretched his arm out to lift the corner of the crate. A huge brown rat scurried out from underneath. It stopped a moment, peaking its nose in the air and sniffing the newcomers. Then it waddled off, apparently uninterested. A shiver squirmed down Joe's spine. "I hate rats," he muttered through clenched teeth.

He tested the crate with his weight, and then stood on it completely. With a slight hop, he hoisted himself up to the concrete-block window sill.

Because the window was so high in the wall, there were no curtains or blinds. He peered into the empty bathroom, then pushed at the bottom of the window. It gave immediately and swung into the room. "I'm in," he called back in a low voice. "Go around to the front and knock."

As Frank left the alley, Joe eased himself through the window and down to the floor. He landed with a soft thud, and a dozen fat black cockroaches scampered into the walls and out of sight. With another shudder, Joe walked into the main room in time to hear Frank's polite—and loud—knock.

Joe quickly let his brother in, then closed and

locked the door. He turned on a light and another dozen or so roaches ran for cover.

The Hardys wasted no time, but searching the room didn't take long, anyway. There wasn't that much to search. They found Doobie's passport, listing him as a citizen of Malta. They found the tool kit with the gray cord. They found some clothes in the dresser. They found a can of race car fuel and a couple of rags in a beat-up suitcase in the closet. And then, under the bed, they found Doobie.

13 Decked by a Neck

Frank spotted it first: a shoe sticking out from under the messy, unmade bed. Then he realized that someone was wearing the shoe.

"Whoa," Joe said in a breathy voice. "Is that what I think it is?"

"I'm afraid so," Frank said. "Don't touch anything." He flipped open his cell phone and dialed 911. The police and paramedics were there in minutes. Frank was glad to see the paramedics working on Doobie.

"Okay, what happened here?" the police officer asked. His badge identified him as Jay Ronald. "Are you friends of this guy?"

"Not exactly," Frank said. "We're journalists covering the race for the *Bayport Herald*. This is D. B.

Poliano, a former racing team owner. A couple of Hugh Conney's mechanics told us Mr. Poliano was staying here, so we came down to get a story."

"And we found him like this," Joe said.

"If he was unconscious when you got here," Detective Ronald asked, "how did you get in?"

"I knocked on the door," Joe said, "but there was no answer—"

"And the door opened, so we just stepped in," Frank concluded. It wasn't really a lie—just a stretch of the truth.

"There's something else you should know," Frank told the officer. "Our hotel room was broken into on Wednesday. Nothing was taken, but we found a gray cord on the desk. Yesterday I rode in the Velodrome cycling race and my bike came apart in the middle of it. The bolts that we recovered had been filed, and I'm sure they're what caused my accident."

The officer listened patiently as Frank continued. "The tool kit on the dresser has a gray cord on it like the one found in our hotel room," Frank said. "The hotel security officer has it." Frank handed Detective Ronald the hotel detective's card. "You might want to contact him and see if there's any connection between the two cords."

Detective Ronald slumped into a mangy-looking chair. "Now why do I think there's more to this story than you're telling me?" He studied Frank's face. "Why would Doobie Poliano sabotage your bike?" the policeman asked. "Are you sure you two came here just to get a story?"

"We were definitely here to get Doobie's story," Joe answered.

"There have been a series of problems at the track lately," Frank said. "As investigative journalists, we've been digging into the case—trying to find out who's behind all these incidents."

"People we've talked to on both the Conney team and the Cristal team mentioned Doobie Poliano as a possible suspect," Frank explained.

"When you search this room," Joe added, "you might find evidence that will back up Poliano as a suspect for the track crimes. I was in Hugh Conney's garage last night when it caught fire. Someone dropped rags burning on race car fuel through the window. There might be evidence in here that would link Doobie to that fire."

"Somehow I have a feeling that you might have already taken a look around yourself," Detective Ronald said, standing up. "But I can't prove it, so you can go." He waved the hotel security officer's card. "I know where to find you if I need to," he said.

The paramedics finally stabilized Doobie's vital signs and quickly wheeled him out to the ambulance. He was still unconscious, and one of the medics said he would need to go into intensive care.

The motel desk clerk wandered over to room 8 after the ambulance left. Oddly enough, he wasn't surprised that an unconscious body had been found in his motel.

It was twelve-thirty when the Hardys started back for the track. While Joe drove, Frank called the hotel security officer and warned him about a possible call from Detective Ronald.

"Okay," Frank said. "It's been a productive morning! I had a few goals: finding out what happened to Manion's cockpit drinking bottle, checking with hotel security about our break-in, and if possible, finding out more about Doobie."

"Done," Joe said. "I'm sure that the police and the hotel detective will figure out that Doobie's the one who broke into our room. They know we're investigative journalists, so they'll make the connection that Doobie was trying to stop us from getting at the truth. "

"The one thing I haven't gotten done yet is find out who had garage seventeen a decade ago at the Melbourne Grand Prix," Frank said.

"The one job I didn't get to yet is pinning down the owner of the Falcon Lake estate," Joe said. "I've got to find out what—or who—ManxInc. is."

"And I'm still going to check out that garage tag just to be sure—wait a minute." Frank took the envelope that Becky had given them out of his gym bag. Inside were the Grand Prix programs from a decade ago, when Doobie was a racing team owner. He shuffled through them. "Here it is!" he said.

"The program from the Melbourne Grand Prix ten years ago." He opened it and leafed through the pages until he found the team profiles. "I've got it. Garage seventeen was assigned to . . . ManxInc."

"You're kidding!" Joe said. "So, that's it. Doobie owns that place at Falcon Lake, and he was going out there because it's his, and—wait a minute. He *couldn't* own that estate. If he did, why would he be staying in the roach motel?"

"Exactly," Frank said. "First we need to back up. All we know about garage seventeen in Melbourne is that it held the team owned by ManxInc. We don't *know* that it has any connection to Poliano."

"But the estate *is* owned by ManxInc. So whoever owns the estate was also a team owner at the Melbourne Grand Prix ten years ago. I have to think about this—and I need some fuel!"

Over lunch in the media section of the stands Frank and Joe watched some of the one o'clock practice session. They had to wear their earplugs to protect their hearing, so they didn't talk much about the case—but each thought about what to do after lunch.

"I'm going to find out some more about Manx-Inc.," Joe said as they left their seats. "I'll start at the media center. There's got to be some record of the company." They heard a Formula One car zoom past them and squeal around hairpin curve nine. "Oh, man, we've got to get this case wrapped up," Joe groaned. "I can't stand being this close to the action and missing all of it!"

"I'm going back to the paddock," Frank said. "I want to talk to Bill about KattTEK and the work it did on Manion's drinking bottle. Don't forget that the Children's Burn Center party starts at six o'clock. And we're supposed to report for our volunteer jobs at four. It's almost one-thirty now, and we need to go to the hotel and change clothes before we go to volunteer. Let's meet here at three."

Frank went to Bill's paddock suite. Using the courtesy phone outside the door, he called upstairs. Bill buzzed him up. There were at least ten other people in the suite. Some were eating lunch, and others were just watching the race cars.

Frank hadn't been there since the party on the night Hugh Conney was arrested. The view from the suite was even better during the daytime, especially with Formula One cars practicing on the track.

"Is Kellam out there?" Frank asked.

"He's in the pits right now," Bill said, "but he'll be back out in a few seconds."

"Joe and I are really looking forward to his qualification run. We feel like we're on his team, even with Manion back. That was kind of a surprise, huh?"

"Yes, and he even confirmed Hugh's story about the nature of their argument," Bill said. "So Hugh is also back on the track."

"I'd like to get some information from you about the drinking bottle in Manion's car. I hear your lab found traces of poison in it. That's what was responsible for Manion's blackout and subsequent crash."

"Yes," Bill said. "It wasn't a lethal dose, but it was enough for him to lose consciousness."

"But somehow it was placed in the bottle before he got in the car," Frank said.

"Not necessarily," Bill pointed out. "The drinking bottle could have been delivered to the garage with the poison already inside. Or the poison could have been placed in the tube in his helmet. In the process of drinking from a straw or a tube, there's automatically some backwashing."

"So it could have been in the tube, and then when he drew in the fluid, some of the poison could have washed back into the bottle."

"That's right," Bill said. He offered Frank a soda, and the two sat in plush club chairs in front of the window that overlooked the track.

"Manion's team is sure that Hugh Conney is responsible for the poisoning," Frank said.

"I hate to say it, but he probably is," Bill answered. "It's got to be someone who knows a lot about how the helmets and the cars work. It's got to be a driver or a mechanic—somebody like that."

"How about an owner?" Frank added. "Some people have told us it might have been Doobie Poliano."

"I heard he was here in town, but I didn't believe it. Then I learned a little while ago that he was found by a couple of journalists in a motel room downtown. They thought he might be dead, but he's not. He's still unconscious, though."

Bill sat up and looked at Frank. "Wait a minute. Those two journalists who found Doobie—they weren't you and Joe, were they?"

"I'm sure the whole story will be on the news this evening, so I might as well tell you. Yeah, we found him."

"Looks like you two are more than feature writers—you're talented investigators."

"Well, I'd better get going," Frank said. "We're working at the Children's Burn Center party."

"Great," Bill said. "We'll be there, of course. It's for a wonderful cause." Bill walked Frank to the door. He reached in the drawer of a small writing desk. "Here's my card. I'll write my personal cell phone number on the back. Feel free to call if you have any more questions about the drinking bottle. And always consider me a resource for your investigations."

"Thanks," Frank said. He glanced at the expensive embossed card and put it in his pocket. Then he left the suite and hurried through the paddock and out to the media center.

Joe was waiting for him outside. "I found Manx-Inc.," he said as they walked to the van. "Well, sort of. It was incorporated in the Bahamas as a blind operation—no owner listed, no officers, directors, indication of the type of business it was—nothing."

"Can you get around that?" Frank asked as he drove them back to the hotel.

"I can," Joe said. "It'll take more time, but I can figure out a way to bypass computer security and find out some more."

The Hardys changed into cargo pants and fresh sweaters. Frank took the KattTEK business card out of his pants pocket and studied it. The logo included an artistic, stylized cat silhouette. He slipped it into one of the pockets in his pants.

The Hardys arrived at the museum right on time. They were blown away by the dinosaur exhibit in the hall where the Children's Burn Center party was being held.

The museum was new, and had a three-story glass-enclosed atrium. The dinosaurs were displayed in a large hall off of the atrium. The exhibit included creatures never seen before in the United States. The most spectacular by far was the Mamenchisaurus. Its neck was thirty-five feet long—half the length of its body. It was so huge that the only logical way to display it was to hang it from the ceiling. It stretched from one corner of the atrium to the other, and continued over the wide staircase that led to the second and third floors.

The Hardys reported to the volunteer coordinator and were assigned to the food crew. The museum was closed to the public at five-thirty, and the rock band arrived at five-forty-five. A bus full of children from the burn center arrived at six o'clock. At six-thirty, various patrons of the center and other city dignitaries arrived.

The party was in full swing by seven. By then several of the drivers, owners, and other Formula One players had arrived. Even though no one seemed ready to leave by ten, that's when the evening had been scheduled to end. The volunteers tactfully began ushering people out when the museum clock struck the hour. Some volunteers left, but the Hardys stayed on as part of the cleanup team.

With the museum nearly empty, the huge atrium echoed with footsteps and the occasional creak of the interior limestone walls. When the lights were turned off, shafts of moonlight sliced through the three-story walls of glass and sparkled along the gently swaying Mamenchisaurus.

Frank took the last tray of cheese cubes to the kitchen. He joined Joe and the others at the long table as they packed up the leftover food.

"Dinosaurs, race drivers, rock music, and kids in recovery," Joe said. "How great is that? My—" He was cut off by the volunteer coordinator.

"Is Frank Hardy here?" she called out.

"Yes," Frank answered, walking over to her.

"You have an urgent phone call. You'll have to take it at the welcome desk. The night guard will meet you there."

Frank walked to the atrium. The guard showed him the phone with the blinking red light, then walked off down the hall.

"Hello?" Frank said into the receiver.

"Don't look up," an obviously disguised voice said through the receiver. "You'll never know what hit you."

Frank immediately looked up. His heart jumped when he saw the seventy-foot-long Mamenchisaurus dancing in the moonlight. It was now swaying faster than it had been before, and hardly looked stable. Within seconds it had completely detached from the ceiling, and several bones were headed right toward him.

Frank felt as if he were in a nightmare. He wanted to run—every impulse in his body urged him to run. But he couldn't make his legs move. He felt stuck to the atrium's floor.

14 Victory Lap

Frank felt rooted to the spot. For a few moments it was very quiet, and he thought his imagination might have gone wild. He wasn't sure the Mamenchisaurus was actually falling. The clattering sound of some of the bones on the floor and the metallic clink of the cables as they snapped against each other confirmed that the nightmare was real.

A large portion of the seventy-foot-long skeleton was plunging right at him. Regaining control of his legs, he zigzagged across the open floor of the atrium, never taking his eye off the bones zooming toward him. He finally reached the staircase and darted underneath it. Crouching, he turned his back to the atrium and waited.

Within seconds the building rocked with the earsplitting sound of the crashing Mamenchisaurus. Pieces of bone—and cement that had been used to fill in the missing fragments—flew around the room like unguided missiles.

Some of the pieces, as big as bowling balls, sailed through the glass walls and out into the parking lot. Some pieces were smaller but dagger sharp. They pierced the limestone walls like arrows.

Even after all the pieces finally landed, snapping and cracking and crumbling noises continued echoing through the three-story room. They were joined by the crisp crunch and crackle of autumn leaves that were now being blown in by the wind through the broken window glass. All of those noises were quickly drowned out by the screech of the security alarm.

Frank finally turned, still in a crouch. Amazingly the dinosaur head and several very long bones were still intact. The rest of the skeleton, however, was a heap of pieces.

Little by little, the six party volunteers who had stayed for the cleanup wandered in and looked around. Everyone was in shock. The night guard ran through the room but stopped when he got to the staircase and saw Frank. He detoured to a locked door, opened it, and reached in to turn off the alarm. Then he returned to Frank.

"I'm happy to see you're all right," he said, relief

washing over his face. "I was worried about you getting caught in this." He shook his head. "What a mess. Some insurance company's going to lose its shirt for this one—unless it was our fault. I sure hope it wasn't."

"Did you call for help?" Frank asked.

"Right away," the guard answered. "As soon as I heard the thing start to give. Everyone in the building's okay, but we need a lot of help securing the building. All that broken glass—and the staircase might be cracked. It's going to take engineers weeks to make sure this building's safe."

"We actually ought to get everyone outside as quickly as possible, just in case anything else happens," Frank pointed out.

"I'm not worried about the bulk of the building," the guard said. "It's been designed to withstand earthquakes and all kinds of natural disasters."

"Well, this is sort of an *un*natural disaster, so it might be a good idea to send everyone else home. Something else could happen. I'll stay to talk to the police when they arrive."

The guard nodded and hurried off to escort the other volunteers to their cars.

"Frank!" Joe ran up and clapped his brother's shoulder. "Man, it's good to see you survived the attack of the Mamenchisaurus."

"Well, he didn't act alone," Frank said. "Come

on—help me find the cables or the connections that bound the skeleton to the ceiling. That baby didn't jump down on his own."

While he and Joe looked for evidence to prove that a human had a hand in the exhibit's collapse, Frank told Joe about the phone call. They continued searching while they talked, but found nothing to show that cables had been cut or connections broken.

Joe looked up at the ceiling. "Come on," he said, bolting up the stairway two steps at a time. "The stairs look like they'll hold. Just keep a grip on the handrail. If the steps go, we'll have something to hang onto."

When they got to the third floor, Joe examined a long groove that ran diagonally across the ceiling. "Look," he said. "That's a track. The Mamenchisaurus was hung as one piece, I'll bet, and manipulated by a computer. Let's find that guard. Didn't I hear him say something about the insurance company and the museum being liable?"

Frank heard sirens in the background. "Yes, he did. The police are almost here," he said. "I'll try to keep them busy as long as I can."

Joe tracked down the guard. He told him he was a computer programmer and could help the guard understand what happened to the Mamenchisaurus.

"I won't touch the program or anything," Joe

said. "That will be great evidence for the police. But if I can just take a look at it, I might be able to explain to you and the museum's attorneys just what happened to make the dinosaur fall."

Joe leaned in closer and lowered his voice. "Depending on how the program shapes up, the museum might not be liable at all—and you'd be a hero."

"Interesting," the guard said. "Okay, but I'm not leaving you alone in there. And you can just look. No touching."

"You got it," Joe said. "But let's hurry. I want to take a look at it before anyone else does."

Frank watched Joe and the guard disappear down the hall, then he turned to the large broken opening in the front window wall of the atrium. He smiled at Detective Jay Ronald as he walked through with a half dozen other policemen.

"Somehow I'm not at all surprised to see you here," Detective Ronald said. "What's your story this time?"

"How's Doobie Poliano?" Frank asked. "Is he still unconscious?"

"Yes, he is—and as you had 'predicted,' we found evidence in his room linking him to the break-in at your hotel and to the fire in Hugh Conney's garage."

"We think he's also the one who nearly strangled my brother outside the same garage the night before. You're sure he's still unconscious, though?"

"Absolutely," the officer said. "He was poisoned, but the doctors think he'll be okay soon."

"Any chance he might have poisoned himself?" Frank asked.

"He was beaten up pretty bad when we found him, but I suppose it's possible. There was no note. Most people who attempt suicide don't stuff themselves under the bed afterward."

"And you're sure he still can't talk?" Frank asked.

"That's right," Detective Ronald said. Frank could tell he was getting impatient. "Okay, investigative reporter, you've done your job. Now let me do mine. Tell me what happened here."

Frank told him the whole story, including the part about the phone call.

"So the dinosaur didn't decide to land on his own," the officer said, gazing at the intact head of the Mamenchisaurus.

"Definitely not," Frank said. "And apparently it *wasn't* Doobie Poliano on the phone—*or* doing whatever it took to disconnect the dinosaur from the ceiling."

"Where's the guard?" Detective Ronald said, looking around. "The weather's really kicking up out there. They're predicting a major storm." With a sigh of relief, Frank saw the museum guard and Joe carefully making their way across the floor.

"Are you through with us now?" Frank asked. "Could my brother and I leave?"

"Yes, but be available for more questions," the officer said.

"No problem," Frank agreed. He and Joe said good-bye and turned the guard over to the detective.

"Come on," Frank said to Joe. "I've got a lot to tell you."

"Me first," Joe said. "I figured out some of this dinosaur mystery. You drive, I'll talk." As Frank drove back to the media center, Joe told him what he'd learned from the exhibit computer program.

"Turns out the whole skeleton was rigged to one track. It could be raised and lowered as one piece and would automatically stop when it reached a certain distance from the ceiling," Joe explained. "Someone could break into the exhibit computer and change the setting for the speed of the descent. Then they could delete the automatic stopping point. All the person would have to do then is start the descent. It would go very fast and wouldn't stop."

"Incredible," Frank said. "And once again we were the specific targets. Someone is definitely trying to get us out of the way—and it's not Doobie Poliano. Not this time."

"Is he still unconscious?" Joe said. Frank nodded and told Joe about his conversation with Detective Ronald.

"I was wondering about that earlier," Joe said. "So he probably has an accomplice. But who?"

Frank pulled into the media center parking lot and turned to face Joe. "Let's retrace a few of our steps," he said. "We suspect that Doobie broke into our room, sabotaged my bike, tried to strangle you outside The Rabbit's garage, was the SUV driver you followed to the estate on Falcon Lake, and set the fire at Hugh's garage."

"We're sure of all those things," Joe said.

"He probably did *not* poison himself, and he *definitely* did not call me to say that he was dropping a dinosaur skeleton on me."

"And if he didn't poison himself, who did? Plus we don't know who might have been behind all the original threats against Hugh and Manion, or who poisoned Manion's fluid, or why Doobie was hanging out at Falcon Lake."

"We can make another assumption," Frank said. "By all reports and his choice of motel, Doobie is *still* not in great financial shape."

"True," Joe said, remembering the rats and roaches.

"So we have to figure that if he's got an accomplice, he's not the one who did the hiring," Frank concluded. "Whoa, feel that wind," he said as the van rocked a couple of times.

"Yeah, looks like that storm is kicking up. Anyway, in other words, you think someone hired Doobie to do the dirty work," Joe said. "Right? That makes sense."

"So we're looking for someone with money, someone with track access, but most importantly, someone with motive," Frank pointed out.

"It can't be either Hugh or Manion, because they've both been badly hurt. So it must be someone else altogether."

"Right," Frank said. "And who has the next best motive after Manion or The Rabbit?"

"The driver who wins if both Hugh and Manion are out? Whoa . . . are you thinking Kellam?" Joe asked.

"I was thinking about this all through the party," Frank said. "Have you noticed how Bill Katt conveniently keeps showing up in this case? He's the eyewitness to the so-called 'kidnapping' of Manion by Hugh. His company is the one that is called on to analyze and identify the poison that caused Manion's crash."

Frank reached into his pocket and took out the KattTEK business card. "Take a look at this," he said.

Joe held it up to the light. "It's pretty cool," he said. "Feels expensive."

"Look closely at the logo."

Joe studied the letters of the name KattTEK, and then followed the silhouette of the cat around the legs, paws, chest, head, and down its back. His pulse sped up a little, and a broad grin spread over his face. He looked at his brother. "This cat has no tail," Joe said, nodding.

"That's because it's a Manx," Frank said, returning Joe's grin.

15 The Final Stretch

"A Manx . . . ManxInc.!" Joe exclaimed. He felt electrified, as if he'd been shocked into the truth.

"So Katt owns ManxInc. and he owns the house out at the lake," Frank said. "An abandoned house in the woods is a great place to meet Doobie and set plans into action. KattTEK is a company that specializes in chemical and biological substance testing and analysis."

"A ready source for poisons for both Manion and Doobie," Joe added.

"He has total access to the track and paddock, and knows all about the cars and the drivers' suits," Frank pointed out.

"The only thing we can't link him to is the

dinosaur drop," Joe said, "but I'd bet my swipe card on it."

"And he's rich enough to pay for it all."

"But not nearly as rich as he'd be if he could knock out the two frontrunners in this race and his team won the Formula One championship," Joe concluded.

"I think we need to meet with Mr. Katt," Frank suggested. He turned over the business card to see Bill's personal cell phone number. "Someplace out in the open, but still private."

He waited a few minutes for Bill to pick up the call, then he spoke. "Hey, Bill. It's Frank Hardy. I just finished having an interesting talk with Doobie, and I'd like to talk to you. Could you meet me in your pit in fifteen minutes?" Frank nodded and hung up.

Joe grabbed their mini video camera, and the teens raced to the paddock. As they ran, they hatched their plan. They swiped themselves in and darted toward the Katt team's pit. The wind was really boisterous now. Papers and trash were whirling around, and Frank had to lean forward a little to keep his footing as he moved ahead.

When they got to the pit, Joe got into the small open tow truck that was standing near the pit wall. He folded himself down and out of sight. Frank walked toward the middle of the pit.

"He's coming," Frank called to Joe in a low voice. Joe turned on the mini video camera and aimed it toward Frank, then stuffed the tiny receiver into his ear. He looked into the viewer. Joe could hear and see everything Frank and Bill said and did. He had to hold the camera very tightly to keep it still in the rocking truck.

"Well, where's your brother?" Bill wondered. "I thought you two were a team."

"Not always," Frank said. "This is one of those times when I prefer to be on my own."

"Talk fast," Bill said. "There's been a tornado sighting just west of here."

"Doobie told me everything, and now that he's out of commission, I thought you might need a new partner." The viewer showed Frank and Bill trying to keep their balance in the fierce wind. The tall lamppost behind them swayed deeply, then bounced back up.

"I don't work with partners," Bill said.

"You might have to change your mind about that," Frank said. "I either go into partnership with you or with Detective Ronald downtown."

"Just what is it that Doobie told you?" Bill said. "You know he's a nut case—has been for years."

"He told me that you were the one responsible for all the initial threats and warnings against Hugh Conney and Manion Cristal, and that you left clues

142

to implicate one or the other." Frank was sure most of his best guesses were on target.

"Doobie read about the threats and decided you had a good idea. He still nursed his grudge against Manion and figured that by adding to the problems that were already occurring he could help bring about Manion's downfall that much sooner."

A powerful swirl of air swept across the track, and for a minute Joe had the horrifying feeling that the truck was about to roll over.

"You poisoned Manion." Joe heard Frank continue. "You gave me three different ways you could have done it, and I'm not sure which you used. But I know that you did it. And once again you successfully implicated Hugh—probably by leaving the same poison in Hugh's suite or in his luggage. Something like that."

"You're guessing," Bill said, but he couldn't seem to resist smiling.

"Somehow you managed to be in the right place at the right time and be an eyewitness to the argument Hugh and Manion had right after Manion checked himself out of the hospital."

"That was a stroke of luck," Bill said. "I was watching Kellam practice from my suite. When I looked across the track, I saw Hugh and Manion under the stands in the infield. They were clearly having a heated argument. Then Manion collapsed and Hugh picked him up and carried him off."

The wind slammed into Bill and Frank. Bill staggered from the impact but managed to hold his footing. "I lost sight of them after that, but I called track security and told them about the incident. I embellished the story, of course."

"On Wednesday night, Joe followed Doobie out to Falcon Lake," Frank said.

"Really?" Bill replied, clearly startled. "You two are even better than I thought."

"We figured out the whole ManxInc. connection," Frank said. "Did you by any chance lend him your garage tag from the Melbourne Grand Prix?"

"The silver triangle? Yes. It was on the key ring that held a spare set of keys to the estate. How did you know about that?"

"He dropped it when he broke into our hotel room to sabotage my bike," Frank answered. "When we discovered Doobie was meeting with you at Falcon Lake, we realized you two were partners."

"We weren't partners," Bill said. "Doobie worked for me. When I found out he was in town, and then a few things happened around here that I had *not* planned, I rightly chose to turn the dirty work over to him."

"Hugh's garage fire, for example," Frank said.

"Yes. Although it was I who nearly strangled your brother the night before. I was surveying the area to see how best to handle the fire. Joe was lurking around, and I hoped to discourage him once and for all. Then I decided to have Doobie actually set the fire. Having Joe and Becky Hannah in the garage at the same time was a bonus I hadn't planned on."

The wind was constantly moving now. It no longer came in sudden gusts, but spun in constant swirls. The tow truck was turned halfway around by one of these swirls, and Joe had to adjust the angle on his video camera.

"I know how you manipulated the dinosaur, too," Frank said, repeating the method Joe had described to him.

"It sounds very complicated, but it was actually fairly easy to do," Bill said. "As a part-time resident of the area, I've managed to get myself onto many boards and committees. Archaeology has always been a passion of mine, so I was one of the committee members who brought the exhibit from China. I was familiar with all the security, as well as the setup of the exhibit."

"Apparently Doobie outlived his usefulness to you," Frank concluded. "You poisoned him and left him to die in the motel."

"What a disgusting place," Bill said. "And now you have outlived your usefulness to me too." He began reaching inside his jacket.

"Don't do anything dumb, Bill," Frank warned.

"I've called the police. I figure if we can't come to an agreement—make a deal right here and now—I'll let them have you."

"And when I tell them about this little meeting, then what?"

"You don't honestly think they'd believe you, do you?" Frank asked.

Again Joe watched Bill reach inside his jacket—but Frank was too quick for him. He head-butted Bill and knocked the man backward off his feet. Joe started the tow truck and backed up.

As Bill regained his balance, Frank delivered a strong right hook to the man's chin. Bill fell to the ground and started to sit back up, but he couldn't make it.

"He's out," Joe said, shaking out his hand. "Let's get him into the truck."

Frank and Joe lifted Bill into the back of the tow truck. With a piece of rope they'd found in the truck, they tied Bill's wrists behind his back. Joe climbed back into the driver's seat, and Frank started around to the passenger side. As he walked, Frank felt a sudden chill, as if the temperature had dropped to freezing. The wind suddenly pushed him away from the tow truck and sent him tumbling into a backward somersault.

He rolled back to his feet about twenty yards from the truck. "The camera," Joe yelled. "Get the camera." Joe was holding Bill's limp body down on the open truck and pointing to the stands.

Frank saw the camera spin through the air. He leaped after it, trying to catch it before it knocked into the ground or any of the debris now whirling around the track.

At last he caught the camera and stuffed it inside his jacket. He turned to race back to the tow truck, but it was gone! He looked through the dust and debris and finally spotted the tow truck on the other side of the pit wall. It was bouncing on the track.

He ran to catch up with it.

"You won't believe it," Joe said. He was still holding Bill down on the open seat. "We flew over here," Joe said. "The wind picked us up, zipped us through the air about a block, and slammed us down on the track!"

"Let's get out of here," Frank said.

"The police should be waiting for us nearby," Joe said. "I called them when you and Bill started to get physical." They drove the tow truck down the pit road and back to the paddock. The police were circling the area, trying to find them.

When Joe told them what had happened to the truck, everyone laughed.

"I see you picked up some major debris," Detective Ronald said, walking around to the truck bed. The wind had finally died down, and the debris was beginning to settle.

"It was Bill Katt all along," Frank said as he and

Joe helped the police remove the tow hook from the rope. "He made all the initial threats to the two drivers and implicated them both."

"And he poisoned Manion," Joe added.

Frank told the police the three methods Bill had suggested for the poisoning: in the bottle, in the water, or in the helmet tube. "I don't know which method he used, but I'm sure you can find out." Then Frank told them what really happened when Hugh and Manion argued under the stands.

"So Manion Cristal's been in Monte Carlo all this time?" Detective Ronald asked.

"Right," Joe said.

"What about Doobie?" the detective asked. "How does he fit into all this?"

Frank told them what the Hardys had learned about Doobie's connection to Bill. "He definitely broke into our hotel room," Frank said. "The implicating evidence was Bill Katt's borrowed garage tag that he left behind. When he learned that Doobie was in town, Bill saw the opportunity to get someone else to do the dirty work and take the heat for it all."

"Exactly," Joe said. "Bill planned the fire in Hugh's garage, but Doobie set it. And just to be really safe, Bill tried to make sure Doobie wouldn't be able to tell his side of the story. Of course, that meant Bill had to pull off the dinosaur crash himself."

Detective Ronald nodded slowly. He looked at Katt, then smiled at the Hardys. "You know, I could tell from our little meeting in that creepy motel that you two weren't *just* investigative reporters. Since then, I've been checking you out. So tell me, how did you get onto Katt in the first place?"

Frank and Joe took turns telling the police how they found out what the silver triangle symbolized and who owned the Falcon Lake estate. "And Bill seemed to know more about some of the incidents than he should have," Frank added.

"When we put together the clues of the garage tag, ManxInc., and the silhouette on the KattTEK business card," Joe concluded, "everything fell into place. All we had to do was get Bill to confirm it."

"And here's your confirmation," Frank said, handing Detective Ronald the video camera. Right on cue, Bill Katt groaned into consciousness.

Two officers helped Katt into one of the police cars and drove off. The Hardys climbed into Detective Ronald's unmarked car for a ride back to their van.

"This place is a mess," Joe observed. Debris had been thrown into countless heaps by the small tornado.

"Looks like opening day will have to be postponed," Frank noted.

"Oh, they'll get the place fixed up pretty quick,"

Detective Ronald assured them. "These kinds of storms are pretty routine around here. It's going to be minor news compared to the big story: 'Hardys Bag Big Katt!'"

She's sharp.

She's smart.

She's confident.

She's unstoppable.

And she's on your trail.

MEET THE NEW NANCY DRE

Still sleuthing,

still solving crimes,

but she's got some new tricks up her sle

NANCY

DREW

girl dete